You'll want to read these inspiring novels by

One Last Wish novels:

Mourning Song • A Time to Die
Mother, Help Me Live • Someone Dies, Someone Lives
Sixteen and Dying • Let Him Live
The Legacy: Making Wishes Come True
Please Don't Die • She Died Too Young
All the Days of Her Life • A Season for Goodbye
Reach for Tomorrow

The Dawn Rochelle Quartet:

Six Months to Live • I Want to Live
So Much to Live For • No Time to Cry

Other Fiction by Lurlene McDaniel:

Angel of Mercy
Starry, Starry Night: Three Holiday Stories
The Girl Death Left Behind • Angels Watching Over Me
Lifted Up by Angels • Until Angels Close My Eyes
Till Death Do Us Part • For Better, for Worse, Forever
I'll Be Seeing You • Saving Jessica
Don't Die, My Love • Too Young to Die
Goodbye Doesn't Mean Forever
Somewhere Between Life and Death
Time to Let Go • Now I Lay Me Down to Sleep
When Happily Ever After Ends • Baby Alicia Is Dying

**From every ending
comes a new beginning. . . .**

Angel of Hope

Lurlene McDaniel

Angel of Hope

BANTAM BOOKS
NEW YORK • TORONTO • LONDON • SYDNEY • AUCKLAND

Published by
Bantam Books
an imprint of
Random House Children's Books
a division of Random House, Inc.
1540 Broadway
New York, New York 10036

Bantam Books is an imprint of Random House Children's
Books. BANTAM BOOKS and the rooster colophon are
registered trademarks of Random House, Inc.

Visit us on the Web! www.randomhouse.com/teens
Educators and librarians, for a variety of teaching tools,
visit us at www.randomhouse.com/teachers

Check out Lurlene McDaniel's Web site!
www.lurlene mcdaniel.com

Library of Congress Cataloging-in-Publication Data
McDaniel, Lurlene.
    Angel of hope / by Lurlene McDaniel.
        p.   cm.
    Summary: After her older sister, Heather, enthusiastic
about changing the world, returns from doing medical missionary work in Uganda, seventeen-year-old Amber, who
feels confused about her future, decides to go to Africa on
the next trip.
    ISBN 0-553-57148-6
    1. Sisters—Fiction.   2. Missionaries—Fiction.
3. Uganda—Fiction.   4. Christian life—Fiction.]   I. Title.
PZ7.M13997   An 2000
[Fic]—dc21   99-046450

RL: 5.9
The text of this book is set in 11.5-point Berling Roman.
Book design by Julie Schroeder
Manufactured in the United States of America
May 2000
OPM 10 9 8 7 6 5 4 3 2 1

To my beloved Mother, who was called home by the angels, and is now reunited with my father forever. See you both when I get there.

Bebe Gallagher
March 1, 1912–September 19, 1999

1

January

Dear Heather,

I hope this letter finds you well rested after your big adventure here in Africa. I also hope you had a blessed Christmas and New Year's Day. We had an especially nice holiday. Visitors on safari, friends of Paul's parents in North Dakota, came through laden with two suitcases full of presents from home. Canned goods, flour, real chocolate chips, peanut butter . . . plus piles of gifts. The boys could hardly believe all their loot, but to their credit, they wrapped up many of the gifts and gave them to the kids here at the Children's Home. It warmed my heart to have them behave so generously. (All without me nagging them either!)

Paul whisked me away for New Year's Eve in Kampala at the Hilton. Decadent woman that I am, I soaked in a hot tub until I turned into a prune. Missionary life in the bush really makes a girl appreciate such goodies as perfumed soap and real shampoo!

I know you're anxious about word of Kia and Alice. Kia continues to blossom—thanks to you. As for baby Alice, well, she's won all our hearts. Both girls are living with us. Yes, it's crowded, but neither is ready to be assimilated into one of the family units yet.

The girls living in the family units are a big help to me with Alice. They take turns feeding her several times a day, plus give her plenty of hugs and cuddling. Unfortunately, Dr. Gallagher says he doesn't feel qualified to repair her palate. So I guess it's up to us and the Good Lord to keep her nourished and healthy until a qualified cranial-facial surgeon arrives from the Mercy Ship when it docks in Kenya this summer. I'm telling you this so that you won't be worried about her—I know how special she is to you.

We all miss you. You're one in a million, a bright and lovely young woman who deserves the best. I pray for you every day, that God will ease the ache in your heart and help you resume your life. Follow your dreams— whatever they may be now.

And give yourself permission to mourn for Ian for as long as you like. There is no time limit on grief, you know. None of us will ever forget you and the brave thing you did for Kia and Alice. Please write and keep us informed of your plans.

In His Love,
Jodene

P.S. Ed Wilson is mailing this for me when he returns to the U.S. He says "Hello" and that you're his hero (heroine) for all time!

Heather Barlow lay on her bed reading and rereading Jodene Warring's letter, memories of Uganda flashing through her mind like postcards. Some images were wonderful: the exotic beauty of the African landscape, the smiling faces of the children at the Kasana Children's Home and hospital, Paul, Jodene, their four children, Heather's friends from the Mercy Ship. Some pictures were frightening: the storm at sea, the sick and dying children in Kenya, her night flight to freedom with baby Alice. And over every picture in her mind's eye, she saw Ian. His smile. His deep blue eyes. She would never see his beloved face again. He would never hold her again and call her "lass" in his rich Scottish accent.

Sadness engulfed her, and she fumbled for his journal on her nightstand. *Thank you, Jodene, for giving this to me*, she thought. She ran her hand across the smooth leather surface. It was all she had of Ian now. All she would ever have. She wiped her teary eyes with the edge of her comforter.

She had spread photographs from her months in Africa on her desk, picking and choosing between the ones she would put on her bulletin board and in her scrapbook. Every face that smiled out at her made her long to turn back the clock and repeat every day of her trip. Against her parents' wishes, she had nixed enrolling at the University of Miami for the winter term. She didn't feel ready to jump back into her life stateside. And Jodene's letter had made her feel even less ready. She felt restless, at loose ends, unable to pick up her life where she'd left off before her mission trip.

A knock on her bedroom door startled her. "Yes?"

"It's me—Amber. Can I come in?"

Heather glanced at her clock radio. Four o'clock. Amber was home from high school, no doubt bursting with trivia she couldn't wait to dump on Heather. "Sure," Heather said, putting the journal aside.

Amber came to the bed and sat on the edge, careful not to disturb the rows of photos. "Still going to the movies with me tonight?"

Heather had totally forgotten her promise

to go out with her sister that evening. "Uh—sure." She held up the letter. "This came from Jodene today. She says Alice can't have her surgery until maybe this summer."

"That's not so far away."

"She needs the surgery now."

"It's not your problem, sis."

"How can you say that? What if everyone took that attitude? Who would take care of these orphans? Someone has to jump in and help, you know. Why not me?"

Amber leaned back and held up a hand. "Hey, I didn't mean to make you mad. I was just saying that she's there and you're here. She'll get the surgery eventually. What else can *you* do from three thousand miles away?"

Heather swung her legs over the side of the bed. "I wanted Mom or Dad to go over and lend a hand. I figured one of them would."

Heather had talked nonstop after returning home, certain she could infect her family with her enthusiasm for Uganda, positive that she could persuade one of her parents, both cranial-facial surgeons, to fly over and perform the necessary surgery on baby Alice. But although her parents had listened intently and praised her work, both had said they were overwhelmed with cases in their practice and couldn't possibly take a leave of absence. Plus, her father was training student doctors in the use of new laser technologies at Miami's medical school. Neither of them could possibly think about doing pro bono work overseas for a year or more.

Her mother had said, "You know your dad and I want to work in the developing world, Heather. My goodness, we spent years in the Peace Corps, so we know how great the need is for skilled volunteer help. And once we retire, we plan to help out plenty, but for now, we can't. We have hundreds of patients who depend on us. We can't just go off and leave them."

Now Amber was sounding as indifferent as their parents. "I don't think you can convince them to go right now," she said. "I think they'd really like to help you out, but they're not going to disrupt their lives just now. Or lose prospective patients."

"They make old people look young again," Heather fired back. "How noble is that? What does it matter if some rich woman gets her face redone when a baby like Alice needs reconstructive surgery to live a better life? And why are you defending Mom and Dad? You're the one who's usually at war with them."

"Well, excuse me if I see their side of the argument. For once I agree with them—you can't expect them to run off to Africa just because you think they should. You're not the only one in the family, you know."

"Well, thank you for your support. But what you're really saying is this is your senior year and you don't want anything to rock *your* boat. If Mom or Dad come to Africa with me, Amber just might be ignored."

"Whoa," Amber said, jumping to her feet. "You are majorly off base. School is perfectly boring and I'm forcing myself to even go to classes until June. This past year hasn't exactly been a picnic for me, you know. Dad's all over me about college in the fall." Amber did an imitation of her father's voice. "'Have you filled out those admission forms yet, Amber?' 'Did you talk to your guidance counselor about the college that's right for you, Amber?'" She threw up her hands. "Has he ever asked once if I even want to go to college? Has he ever thought I might like to get a job and earn some bucks?"

"Get real. Of course you're going to college."

"You're not."

"But I will."

"When?"

"Trying to get rid of me?" Where did Amber get off, trying to make her feel guilty about taking some time to figure out what she wanted to do with the rest of her life? Amber had no idea what Heather had been through during the past six months. "What would you spend the money on, anyway? Your closet is already overflowing."

"Well, maybe everyone isn't cut out to save the world like you are. Maybe I'd like to have a good time before I grow old and die."

Exasperated with Amber's self-centered attitude, Heather said, "At least you have the opportunity to grow old. I met kids in Africa who'll never grow old. They'll be dead from AIDS or TB or malaria before they get out of their twenties."

"Then maybe I'll just sit around my room and feel sorry for myself like you do."

"Out," Heather said, pointing to the door. "This is my room and I don't need you sniping at me."

"I'm on my way. And forget about coming to the movies with me tonight. I'd hate to take you away from your pity party."

Heather slammed the bedroom door as soon

as Amber had walked out. Then she sat and seethed. What was the matter with her family? Didn't anyone understand what she was going through? Especially Amber. Her sister had always looked up to her, come to her for advice. Now they were at each other's throats. Why couldn't Amber understand how the past six months had affected Heather's life?

She threw herself across her bed, scattering the photographs across the floor. She didn't care. Amber was correct about one thing: Heather couldn't return to Africa and make everything right for Alice. At the moment she couldn't even make everything right for herself.

Her gaze fell on Ian's diary and her heart lurched. "Why, Ian? Why?" she asked aloud. What had it all been about? Why had she given everything in her heart to the missionary journey aboard the Mercy Ship and to Uganda, only to have it all snatched away? It made no sense. And she didn't have Ian to talk to about it either. She was going to have to go it alone.

Alone. The word sent a shiver down her spine.

Heather buried her face in her pillow and began to cry.

2

"Why are you acting antisocial today, Amber?"

Amber raised her eyes from the mush on her food tray and looked at Dylan Simms. "I'm in the dumps and didn't want to inflict myself on anybody else."

"I'm your guy, remember? You're supposed to tell me when you've got a problem." Dylan slid into the empty chair beside Amber at the table she'd chosen on the far side of the cafeteria. "So, did you and your old man go at it again?"

Amber stuck her fork upright into her mound of mashed potatoes. "Believe it or not, I got into it with Heather yesterday afternoon."

"Your sister? The Queen of Good-Deed-Doers?"

"Hey, show some respect."

Dylan held up his hands. "Sorry. It's just a surprise, that's all. You've only spoken of her in worshipful tones until now."

Amber made a face. "Do you want me to talk about it, or do you want me to dump my tray in your lap?"

"Talk. Please. I can't do this menu twice today." He rested his chin in his palm.

"We had a big fight, and she must have been really angry because she didn't come downstairs for dinner. She was asleep when I left for school, but I'm positive she's still mad at me."

"What happened?"

"You know how I've told you what a hard time she's having coming back to her real life from Africa." Dylan nodded. "Well, she had been doing better, but then yesterday she got this letter from the missionaries she lived with over there and it set her off again. She's totally fixated on that little baby she helped get out of Sudan. She acts as if unless she does something personally to help the baby, the baby will die. And if the baby dies, Heather's going to feel as if it's all her fault."

"And you said . . . ?"

"I told her to get over it. There was nothing more she could do. It was time for someone else to take over the project. She wants Mom or Dad to drop everything and zip over to Africa and operate on the baby—which neither one can do. Heather's sore at me because I actually see their side. I know she thinks I'm insensitive. I'm not, but there's only so much one person can do. She's got to realize that she can't fix everything that's wrong."

"You've always told me the two of you were different."

"I don't want to go out and save the world like she does. I know my limits."

"Her thing isn't your thing. And that's why I love you—you're fun. We have fun together. Blow off your funk, girl. I'll take you out tonight. That'll make you feel better."

"You know Dad won't let me date on a school night."

"So sneak out. You have before."

Amber sent him a sideways glance. She could tell by his expression that he had lost interest in her problems. "I don't want to sneak out. I want to get things right with my sister."

She watched Dylan's gaze drift toward a group of his baseball buddies coming through the door. He waved them over.

"I'm talking here," Amber said irritably,

wishing he'd be more sensitive to her feelings. "Can you give me a few minutes?"

"Yeah, sorry. So you want to meet me someplace tonight?"

"Didn't you hear me the first time? No, I don't."

Dylan patted her hand. "Look, Amber, from what you've told me about your sister, all you have to do is say you're sorry. She's probably dying to forgive you."

Dylan's friends stopped at the table, and Dylan stood and started talking to them. Amber suddenly felt like excess baggage. It was usually that way when Dylan's friends came around. She had once accused him of wanting to be with them more than he wanted to be with her, which he'd denied. She sighed. There would be no getting his attention back. She knew too well what would happen next— the guys would talk, Dylan would make an excuse to leave, and they'd wander off in a herd.

Minutes later he asked her, "Mind if I bug out?"

"Be my guest. I was alone before you came over here, remember?"

She watched him saunter off and wondered what good it was to have a boyfriend if he wasn't around when she needed him. His juvenile buddy bonding was frustrating enough, but he'd practically ignored her concerns about Heather. Amber's already crummy day had turned crummier. In truth, Heather's time in Africa had changed her *and* her relationship with Amber. There was a wall between them that Amber didn't know how to scale, and although Heather had shared her adventures with her family, Amber got the impression that there was much she hadn't shared.

For starters, Ian McCollum, the medical missionary Heather had cared deeply about and lost so horribly, was rarely discussed. Just the mention of his name brought tears to Heather's eyes, as did the photographs of the two of them together. Heather practically slept with his journal under her pillow, reading and rereading it. Growing up, Amber and Heather had shared everything, but not this. Amber felt shut out and cut off.

She came home to the aroma of freshly baked chocolate chip cookies. She called out for the housekeeper, then remembered it was Dolores's day off. Walking into the kitchen, Amber found Heather removing a cookie sheet from the oven. "What's this? You baking?" she asked, genuinely surprised. Most afternoons Heather was hidden away in her room.

"Peace offering," Heather said with a quick smile. She set the cookie sheet on the marble-topped island in the center of the kitchen. "I was rude and nasty to you yesterday, so I thought I'd bake my way back into your good graces."

Amber fished a piping hot cookie from the sheet and blew on it. "Good choice. You know I can't resist anything chocolate." She bit into the cookie, savoring the rich, buttery taste as much as Heather's apology. "But you didn't have to bake me cookies. Although I'm glad you did. I was all set to tell you I was sorry too. And I am, Heather. I didn't mean to sound like I don't care about baby Alice. I do care. But mostly because you care about her. Understand?"

"Perfectly." Heather pulled off her oven mitt and gave Amber a hug. She stepped back to the counter and began moving the warm cookies to a plate. "It's a little like looking at those magazine ads with pictures of hungry children. Sure the photo tugs at your heart, but it's easy to close a magazine and forget the picture. But when you actually see the baby, when you hold her in your arms, you've got a memory. Whenever I shut my eyes, the memory comes calling. Do you know, I can still feel the weight of little Alice just like I was holding her? I can still remember how she looked when she smiled up at me. Her little eyes lit up, and in spite of her birth defect, I knew she was happy. Of course I saw hundreds of needy children, but I truly made a difference for Alice and her sister. I know how important being close to a sister is."

Amber nodded, feeling a mixture of sympathy for the baby and shame that she hadn't grasped the true depth of Heather's feelings toward her. "I guess I expected you to be the same sister I remembered growing up with instead of the one who came back from Africa."

"Well, I'm not the same sister. I'm the one who watched babies die just because they couldn't get to a doctor in time. I'm the one who saw mothers abandon their children because they couldn't take care of them. Many people in our country take life for granted. No, worse . . . they think life is a guaranteed right.

Of course we have poverty here, but not as overwhelming and widespread."

Amber listened, unsure of how she was supposed to respond. She hadn't experienced what her sister had, but Heather had gone through what Amber now was going through— a dull senior year of high school and apprehension about her future. Amber kept hoping that Heather would remember that she herself had been feeling much the same way this time last year before she took off to Africa. Still, she thought it best not to bring that up now. "I'm glad you're home," she ventured. "I missed you. And I'll try to be more sensitive to the new Heather."

"I missed you, too. And I don't mean to act so serious all the time. Besides, I had a pretty good day. A friend called me, Boyce Callahan. We were on the mission trip together."

"You wrote about him in your e-mails. You said he had a thing for your Swedish roommate, Ingrid."

"That's history," Heather said with a wave of the spatula. "Ingrid is dating her old boyfriend again, and Boyce is back in class at the University of Alabama. Talking to him today brought back good memories. He was always cracking jokes and making us laugh. And he was nuts about peanut butter. Did I ever tell you that?" Amber shook her head. "He feels a lot like I do—life is tame and dull by comparison after Uganda."

"I guess Miami and your old life can never compete again," Amber mused, feeling a pang of jealously.

"Probably not."

Heather had no idea how much her answer stabbed at Amber's heart. Amber knew she should feel glad because Heather had found such dedication and zeal in her life, but right now she felt only envy because Heather's world was so much bigger than hers. And yet there was no way Amber was ever going to sail off to Africa to capture the dreams that had given her sister such a sense of purpose.

Amber held out a cookie. "I'm hogging these. Don't you want some? I'll pour us both some milk."

"No, thanks." Heather wrinkled her nose. "My stomach's been bothering me."

"Too bad. More for me." Amber scooped up two more cookies and headed to the refrigerator for milk.

"Plus I'm too excited to eat," Heather added.

Amber paused and turned. "What?"

"Boyce is studying engineering at 'Bama, and he told me he can shave off a semester of school if he participates in a work program. He says he's already talked to the head of the department and the professor has agreed to endorse Boyce's plan to the dean."

Great . . . one more person with a life, Amber thought. "And the plan is . . . ?"

"He's returning to Uganda in March."

"Good for Boyce. What's that got to do with you?" Amber asked, suddenly suspicious of Heather's smug smile.

"One way or another, I'm going with him."

3

"Heather, you can't be serious!" Dr. Ted Barlow exclaimed at the dinner table that night after Heather had revealed her plan.

Dr. Janet Barlow set her fork down on the plate with a clink. "You're supposed to be choosing a college, not talking about running off to Africa again. It's time to get on with your life, honey."

Amber sat silent, in total agreement with their parents. She'd been in shock ever since Heather had told her about her plan to return to Uganda. She didn't want Heather to go so far away again. Amber wanted her sister close by, to talk to, to help with her own problems.

Heather considered her parents thoughtfully. "No disrespect, but I'll be nineteen in April. Of course I can return if I want to. I know Jodene and Paul will give me a place to stay. And Dr. Gallagher will be ecstatic to have an extra pair of hands helping in the hospital."

"That's what you want to do with your future?" Janet asked. "Work in a Third World hospital? If it's hospital work you want, your father and I can get you any number of jobs right here in Miami while you attend college."

"It's not about working in a hospital. It's about working in *that* hospital—the one in Uganda. This isn't about me, Mom. It's about them—the kids in Uganda. Boyce is designing and building an irrigation system on the property belonging to the Children's Home. Getting water to the back acreage will allow the kids of the village to expand their living quarters fivefold. That means the home can open itself up to even more orphans. They'll learn to farm and sell their crops and support themselves. I can help with setting up a small clinic for the girls, screen them for serious illness, give immunizations. It's a wonderful plan, and I want to be a part of it. The sooner I get there, the more I can help."

Her parents exchanged glances.

"Honey," her mother began, her tone sympathetic, "I know how difficult it is to come down from the high of the kind of adventure you had in Africa. When I first returned from the Peace Corps, the last thing I wanted to do was begin medical school. But your grandfather insisted, and I'm glad he did. I might never have gotten my medical degree if I hadn't begun classes when I did."

"We enrolled in med school together. It offered us another kind of adventure," her father added with a wink at his wife. "Heather, listen to us. You're intelligent, and you have so much potential. You can do anything you set your mind to. Don't waste the opportunities we can give you. Go to college, get a degree. Then, if you still want to return to Africa, go with our blessings."

"But I want to go now," Heather said, shoving her plate to one side, the food hardly touched. "You always told Amber and me that the years you spent in Central America were life-changing. You told us that one day you'd go back and use your surgical skills to help the poor. Well, here it is, years later, and you've never gone."

"First we wanted to get you girls raised," her mother said. "We wanted the two of you to have a normal life—go to college, get a leg up in the world—before we ventured off."

"Do you know what I think?" Heather didn't wait for an answer. "I think you've gotten too comfortable. You've forgotten your dreams, your ideals. You've sold out."

"That's uncalled for," Ted said, tossing his napkin on the table. "We've worked hard to build our reputations in this community with both our peers and our patients. It's our hard work that enabled you to run off to Africa in the first place. Remember, you had to raise all your own funds to secure a place on that Mercy Ship. If I recall, I simply wrote a check for your portion. So don't act as if we've somehow abandoned the world's underprivileged simply because we aren't packing our bags and heading off to do charity work."

"I've never acted ungrateful for all that the two of you have done for me," Heather said quietly. "And I'm not trying to put a guilt trip on either of you. I'm simply reminding you that the two of you are the reason I wanted to go on the trip in the first place. Your stories about your days in the Peace Corps have inspired me all my life. I thought you'd be pleased that I want to follow in your footsteps."

Janet reached across the table for Heather's hand. "Of course we're pleased, honey. To have a child who's acting as socially responsible as you do is a point of real pride for your father and me. It's just that we're confused about why you don't enroll at the university as you once talked about doing. One trip to Africa shouldn't change goals you've had all your life."

Amber bit her tongue to keep from jumping into the argument. While she didn't want Heather to wander off to Africa, her sister did have a point. It was her life and she should be able to do what she wanted with it. Amber was almost ready to say something in Heather's defense when Heather spoke.

"The trip wasn't at all what I expected. The things that happened to me last summer changed me and my goals. I met missionaries who were interested in the condition of people's souls, not just in their physical well-being. They're giving people a stake in eternity, a hope beyond this life. Maybe I'm not explaining it very well, but I know I'm different than when I left. I see a bigger picture now. A higher good. And that's the thing I want to reconnect with in Uganda. That's the main reason I want to go back."

"You had a religious experience?" Her father looked incredulous. "Is that what you're saying? You want to put your life on hold because you felt something spiritual?"

"Why is that so weird?" Amber could no longer keep quiet. "Maybe Heather's right. Maybe there's more to life than making money and telling your kids what they should do with their lives."

All eyes turned her way. She squared her jaw.

"I don't see you doing anything especially productive, young lady," her father said. "You're graduating in June and you haven't filled out a single college application. Do you think some college is going to take you simply because you wear good clothes? Which, by the way, you spend plenty of my money on."

"Heather's right," Amber shot back. "You two have sold out. What's important to you isn't important to us."

"Well, this is just great." Ted threw up his hands. "Neither one of our daughters wants to take advantage of the things we've worked for all our lives to give to them."

"Now, Ted, no one said that," Janet said.

"*I* said it." He shoved his chair away from the table, stood, and looked hard at Heather and Amber. "Tell you what—the two of you come up with a game plan and start paying for it yourselves. Heather, a plane ticket to Africa should cost in the neighborhood of a thousand dollars. Amber, when you graduate, get a job. Since the two of you are so intent on making your own choices for your lives, you can pay your own way." He walked out of the room.

Janet sighed and looked at both girls. "Listen, your father's upset. I'll talk to him."

Heather leaned toward her mother. "You understand, don't you, Mom? You heard what I was trying to say, didn't you?"

"Yes. But I'm not sure I agree. You aren't qualified in medicine. You aren't qualified in theology. If feeding people body and soul interests you, go to school and get some training in both fields. Then you'll be able to contribute something worthwhile."

"What about on-the-job training?" Amber interjected. "Isn't that valuable too?"

"Amber, your experiences in life don't weigh nearly as much in my book as your sister's, so your future plans consist of attending college in the fall. Get used to it. Go to your school counselor and start filling out applications tomorrow." Janet turned back to Heather. "Your heart's in the right place. It always has been, but you must honestly evaluate the best way to follow your heart. Your father and I are asking you to explore all your options before making a commitment. That's all."

"I have a better idea, Mom." Heather leaned forward eagerly. "Come with me. Just for a few months. See for yourself. Chase your dream again—the one that inspired you in the Peace Corps. After we've worked in Uganda side by side, if you still can't see the value in what I want to do, I'll come home and enroll at the University of Miami. That's a promise." She settled back in her chair, her hands held out beseechingly. "What do you say? Will you come with me?"

"Well, tonight went over like a lead balloon." It was later in the evening, and Amber was sulking in Heather's room, still angry about the way her mother had ordered her around. Didn't she have any say-so in her own life?

"Dad *was* pretty mad," Heather said. Their father had gotten a call from the hospital and had hurried off to stitch up the face of a car accident victim. "I wish I could make him understand my point of view."

"How about Mom? She gets it, but she treats

both of us like we're still babies. She'll never go to Africa. You're wasting your breath."

"She didn't say no." Heather lay on her bed, staring up at the ceiling. "All I want her to do is seriously think about coming with me."

"You mean you're still planning to go?"

"Yes."

"What about the money? You know when Dad says something, he means it."

"I have a savings account. This trip will clean it out, but so what? That's what a savings account is for."

Amber had no extra money, having recently bought a new stereo system for her car. Now she wished she hadn't. "I'm broke, so I guess I really will have to go to work," she said glumly.

"The other day you told me you might get a job when you graduated instead of going to college. Now you sound as if it's a prison sentence. What changed?"

"A job became Dad's idea," Amber confessed.

Heather giggled. "Fickle girl. Listen to your big sister. Go to college. You've got no good reason not to. Plus, Dad will pay for it."

"It's not that I don't want to go, it's just that I'm burned out with school, and the thought of facing four more years of studying books gives me a headache."

"Lots of frat parties," Heather teased.

"Don't you know? My life's one big party," Amber said glumly. "I feel like I'm standing on the outside looking in on other people's lives. Like I'm watching a movie where everyone's busy and having fun except me. All my friends have plans for their lives. I don't know what I want."

"You could come meet me in Africa when school's out. There's plenty for you to do over there."

"First Mom, then me. Soon you'll persuade Dad to go and we'll *all* be over there building huts and nursing sick kids."

"There are worse things than doing good for others, sis. I'm going, and if anyone wants to go with me, they'll be welcome." Heather stretched as she lay on the bed. "But right now I'm throwing you out of my room and crashing. My stomach's killing me and I'm tired to the bone."

Amber rose to leave. From the bed Heather added, "But think about what I said about coming to Africa with me. You just might begin the adventure of your life."

4

Saturday night Amber went to a party with Dylan at the home of one of his friends. The luxurious houses faced an inland waterway that cut through sections of Miami Beach. Expensive late-model cars spilled out of the driveway, across the lawn, and down the street. Music roared from poolside speakers, although no one was swimming on the chilly February night, and inside the house cigarette smoke hung like a pale curtain. With his arm possessively around Amber's waist, Dylan dragged her from group to group of their high-school friends. After an hour she disengaged herself and said she was going to the bathroom. Instead, she went out onto the patio and breathed deeply. The fresh, cool air helped clear her head. She wished she'd never come to the party.

She couldn't think about having a good time after the bombshell her mother had dropped that morning. Janet had strolled into the kitchen, where Amber and Heather were having breakfast, and said, "Heather, I'm going to Africa with you."

Heather, who was toying with her food, jumped up. "You are? Honest? Why did you change your mind?"

"Your father and I talked well into the night when he returned from the hospital, and we agreed that anything that was this important to you should be important to us, too. Most people your age are trying to get away from their parents, but you want me with you. I should be flattered instead of telling you no."

Heather flew across the kitchen and threw her arms around her mother. "But your practice—you said—"

"I know what I told you at Christmas, but I've made some arrangements over the past few days. Your father will take over some of my cases, and Dr. Liberman will handle the others. None of my patients will lack care. And besides, I won't get rusty. I intend to perform surgeries while I'm in Uganda. I'll begin with fixing that little baby's cleft palate."

Heather started crying. Amber sat in stunned silence, feeling as if a door had been slammed in her face and she'd been left standing out in the cold.

"Mom, this is—is wonderful," Heather stammered. "I—I'm overwhelmed."

"I talked to Ned Chase—you may remember him, he's a colleague. Anyway, he and his wife, Britta, donate six weeks every year to an organization called FACES. It's a network of cranial-facial surgeons who donate their time and talents to helping in developing nations. Ned practically burst with enthusiasm when I told him what you wanted me to do. He's also connected me with the organization, which will help clear away red tape. You know, I can't simply waltz into Uganda and start operating without special sanction. The FACES group will handle the details for me."

"That's fabulous! Can we get it all done by March first?"

Janet smiled. "Probably not that soon. I have some loose ends I can't tie up before then." When Heather looked crestfallen, her mother added quickly, "But certainly we'll leave by April first."

"I'll write Jodene and tell her the good news.

She'll be really happy to know that Alice is going to get the best surgeon in the world."

Janet laughed. "I'm not the best in the world, but I will do my best."

"You're the best to me," Heather said. She gave her mother another hug and hurried out of the kitchen.

Amber sat in stonelike silence.

"You don't seem overjoyed," Janet said. "Do you have a problem with our plans?"

Amber shrugged, not trusting her voice.

"I'll only have a six-week visa, Amber. I think you and your father can tough it out for six weeks, if that's what's bothering you."

Amber said, "I could care less," pushed aside her unfinished breakfast, and left the room.

Now, recalling the morning in vivid detail, she wished she'd said all that had been on her mind when she'd had the chance. She felt like an afterthought instead of a real member of the family. Heather's needs, Heather's wishes, always came before Amber's. Not that she wanted to go down the same road as Heather, but she did want—had always wanted—the respect for her own thoughts and plans that Heather received for hers. Her parents treated her like a baby, and she hated it.

"There you are." Dylan's arrival on the porch broke Amber's reverie. "Why'd you run off?"

"I didn't run off. I wanted some fresh air."

"I've been looking all over the place for you." He sounded irritated.

"What? I have to check in with you when I want to escape the smog in there?"

"No, but you could have mentioned you were going outside."

"Would you have even heard me?" She didn't wait for his answer. "Listen, Dylan, I don't need a lecture from you about reporting in on my whereabouts. My father gives them to me often enough."

"Well, excuse me for caring."

"About me?" She scoffed. "What you care about is not losing face in front of your buddies. Wouldn't want them to think you don't have control of your woman."

"Hey, knock it off." His face reddened. "Look, lately you've been a real b—"

"Don't say it," Amber warned.

"You haven't been one bit of fun ever since your sister got home from Africa. You're all uptight. And mad at the world. Maybe it would have been better if she'd never come home."

Amber balled her fists and stepped towards

him. "Don't you dare say anything bad about Heather. I missed her like crazy and I'm glad she's home. She could have died over there, you know."

"Yeah, well, she didn't. But you're acting like *somebody* died."

"Kids die over there every day. As if you care."

"And you do?"

He'd hit a sore spot, and she resented it. "Heather does," she said. "That's good enough for me."

Dylan looked confused. "What are we arguing about here? I'm trying to be sympathetic toward your crummy moods, and you're cutting me off at every turn. Are you—you know—having that PMS thing?"

She rolled her eyes. "Oh, grow up." Earlier she'd thought she would tell him about her morning and the shock she'd felt at her mother and Heather's decision to take off to Africa together. But now she didn't want to tell him anything. She crossed her arms. "Let's just forget the whole thing. There's no way I can explain it all to you, and besides, we came here to party, not stand around on the porch talking."

"Hey, that's more like it. That's the Amber I

remember . . . my party girl." He put his arm around her.

"That's me," she said, forcing a smile and allowing him to lead her inside. Dylan stayed next to her the rest of the evening, refusing to run off with his friends to buy more beer when they asked. Yet despite Dylan's presence, despite all the noise, music, and laughter, Amber felt as alone as if she were stranded on the moon—far away and looking down on a scene that she didn't want to be a part of, in a crowd she felt would never understand her. How could they? She couldn't understand herself. All she knew was that there was a void widening every day, setting her apart from them and the world of high-school popularity she'd once coveted.

"I don't know what's wrong with me," Amber told Heather days later. She had decided to try to explain her inner turmoil to her sister. She'd missed their long heart-to-heart talks, and if Heather was heading to Africa, Amber might not be able to talk to her face to face for months. "I mean, I have everything I ever thought I wanted. I have tons of friends, a boyfriend—Dylan's one of the most popular guys in school. I have a car, clothes coming out the wazoo—Dad's right about that much. But some days I hate getting up and going to school and pretending life is fabulous when it isn't."

The afternoon had turned warm, and they were out by the pool, dangling their legs in the bright turquoise water. Heather stared into the water, making lazy circles beneath the surface with her toe. "You've got a lot going on deep down," she said. "You have it all, but you're mixed up, unhappy, feeling like no one understands you, no one *wants* to understand you, and yet you're supposed to make life-altering decisions while you're in this state of turmoil. Is that about it?"

"That's exactly it. I know I'm supposed to be grateful—and I am," Amber added hastily. "But, jeez, is this all there is?"

"If you could do anything in the world, have anything in the world, what would you want?"

"You mean besides fame and fortune without having to put myself out for it?" Amber sobered and stared hard at the cool water. "I don't know, sis. I just don't know."

"Do you want to marry Dylan?"

"Yuck! No way."

Heather laughed. "He doesn't seem so horrible."

"He's all right. But he acts like a jerk sometimes. He throws temper tantrums if everything doesn't go exactly his way, or if I don't want to tag along with him and the gang to some mindless party. And sometimes I don't want to."

Heather continued to make circles in the water with her foot. "How about a job? Maybe if you worked for a while it would help you zero in on something else."

"And what kind of a job can I get just out of high school? I sure don't want to lean out a window and ask, 'Do you want fries with that burger?' a million times a day."

Heather punched Amber playfully. "There's always retail. You love clothes. Maybe you can get a job in a store selling clothes."

Amber rolled her eyes. "Oh, sure. And see every fashion mistake in the city walk in and out the door. How could I tell some girl that a dress looks fabulous on her when it doesn't?"

"Mom and Dad have tons of friends. You could get an office job."

"Doing what? Sorting mail? Making the lunch runs for the other workers?"

"There's the hospital."

"Eek! I pass out at the sight of blood."

"You do have a problem, sis."

"You think I'm useless too, don't you?" Amber's gloom deepened.

"No. I think you just haven't discovered your passion yet. I was lucky. I've known ever since the fifth grade what I want to do."

"You want to save the world," Amber said, feeling envious because Heather's dreams were happening. And Heather's dreams won a high approval rating from all who heard them. Helping sick and hungry children was noble.

"I learned that I can't save the whole world," Heather confessed, her expression enigmatic. "Still, I want to do whatever I can to help. That's why I'm going back. I can help these orphans."

"I'd give anything if I felt that way."

"Sometimes you have to do it before you feel it."

Amber sighed. "Maybe you're right. Maybe I should go to Africa with you."

"You could, you know."

Amber studied Heather's face. "You're serious, aren't you?"

"Very serious."

"I can't see that happening. Dad would pitch a fit."

"And there is the problem of your final

couple of months of classes. You are going to graduate, aren't you?"

"Of course. It's just so boring, I can barely stay awake. One of my teachers calls it senioritis."

"I had it too," Heather admitted. "Every senior gets it. This time last year, all I could think of was my upcoming trip on the Mercy Ship. It pulled me through my slump."

"If only I had something to look forward to like that."

Heather patted Amber's hand sympathetically. "I've invited you to Africa. It beats passing out burgers and fries."

"And don't think I'm not worried about it. Dad may have let you back into his good graces, but I'm still in the doghouse."

"He'll ease up on you once we're gone."

Amber wanted to beg Heather not to go, but just then the phone rang. She hurried to answer it, making wet footprints on the stone patio.

"Kelly here," her friend's voice announced.

"What's up?"

"Bad news, I'm afraid. Dylan asked Jeannie Hightower out and she said yes. I thought you should know."

5

Amber felt herself go hot and cold. "So?" she asked, keeping her voice controlled.

"Well, everybody knows you and Dylan have been together for months. And now all of a sudden he asks Jeannie out. What's going on? Did you two break up?"

Amber heard Kelly pause, no doubt waiting for an explosive reaction. Refusing to give her one, Amber said, "Maybe it's a study date. They're in the same calculus class."

"Some study date. Jeannie told Brooke that Dylan's taking her to a movie."

"And you believe Brooke? You know she just talks to hear her own voice."

"I checked it out with Liz. She said it was true."

Liz was Dylan's freshman sister, so the story probably was true. "It's a free country," Amber said. "I guess he can date whomever he wants." She was reeling on the inside, but she was determined not to let Kelly know. If she fell apart over the news, the gossip mill would have a field day.

"Did something happen between you two?" Kelly tried again to pry information from Amber.

"Nothing that I recall."

"How about at the party Saturday night? You were outside talking for a long time—"

"Look, Kelly, nothing happened. And I really could care less what Dylan does and who he does it with. I have more important things on my mind." By now Amber's hand ached from gripping the receiver so tightly. "But thanks for the update. Where else could I have heard such news except from a friend?"

The subtle insult passed unnoticed. Kelly said, "Um—well, okay. Just so long as you aren't hurt, I guess it's no big deal."

Amber's only satisfaction was hearing the disappointment in Kelly's voice over her non-reaction. "It's no big deal," she echoed, and hung up.

She stood shaking with anger, holding the receiver, for a long time. Dylan was dumping her. And he didn't even have the guts to tell her to her face. "So what!" she said aloud. "I was bored with him anyway." She stalked off, making it to her room before she started to cry.

Amber didn't want to return to school the next day but knew she had to in order to save face. As long as she pretended not to care, the gossip mill wouldn't have as much to talk about. One crack in her facade would ruin everything. She felt the gaze of her classmates on her as she walked down the hall or entered a classroom. And when she saw Dylan and Jeannie huddled in a corner of the cafeteria, she almost caved. All she wanted to do was deposit her food tray on their heads.

A pop quiz in chemistry added to her misery. By the time she arrived home, she had a headache and a need to punch something. She went to the gym room at home and worked out with a kickboxing tape. The wall of mirrors told her she wasn't very good at it, but after forty-five minutes of kicking and thrusting, she felt better.

She was running on the treadmill when Heather found her. "I wondered where you were. Everything okay?"

"No." Amber turned off the machine and sank to the floor, her back braced against a wall. "It's been a crummy day." She told Heather what had happened, all the emotion gone out of her.

"You told me Dylan wasn't that important to you. Was that the truth?"

"He wasn't. It's just that I've always been the dumper, not the dumpee."

"So your pride's hurt. Is that it?"

Heather had settled next to her on the floor, and Amber looked sidelong at her. "It's just one more thing to add to my list. You see, that's the problem—no one thing is huge, but added all together, my life is nowhere."

"You're positive you're not really broken up about Dylan. You've dated him a long time. You used to tell me about how much fun you two had together."

"That was a lifetime ago."

"You never loved him?"

"I don't love him. Why the third degree?"

Heather picked at a thread on the carpet. "Did you ever . . . ? Well, have you and Dylan ever . . . ?" She left the questions hanging.

Amber wiped perspiration on a towel. "Did I ever go all the way with him? Is that what you want to know?"

Heather's face turned red. "It's none of my business. I shouldn't have asked."

"The answer is no. I could have. He asked me plenty of times, but I never did."

"That's good."

"I sure think so now. How about you?" Heather shook her head. "Not even with Ian?"

Tears filled Heather's eyes, and Amber regretted prying. Still, Heather chose to answer. "The first time I kissed him was also the last time I kissed him. We stood in the moonlight together under the skies of Africa. He held me and he kissed me. He told me he loved me. I was too overwhelmed to say 'I love you' back to him. I thought I'd have all the time in the world to tell him how much I loved him. I thought I'd kiss him a hundred more times. But I didn't.

"I've never been sorrier about anything in my life. I should have told him how I felt when I had the chance. I had one chance, and one chance only. Then it was gone. Then *he* was gone." Heather took a deep, shuddering breath. "That's why I asked you about Dylan. If you really care for him, fight for him. Don't let your pride stand in the way of telling someone you love him and want him back."

Tears welled in Amber's eyes as she felt the depth of Heather's pain and loss. They made her own problems suddenly seem petty. Many times she had wished that Heather would talk to her about Ian. Now that she had and Amber saw how raw and open the wound was on her sister's heart, she realized that to have discussed Ian carelessly would have lessened what he and Heather had shared. Amber clasped Heather's hand. "I've never felt that way about Dylan. I've never felt that way about anyone. I wish I could have met Ian. He must have been very special to have snagged my sister's heart so completely."

Heather wiped her eyes and gave a self-conscious laugh. "I didn't mean to get carried away. You were talking about your problems and I butted right in with mine. Sorry. I remember how stupid high school can be at times. But by June it will be behind you. You'll have something else going on and high school will be a memory."

"And by June you and Mom should be heading back from Africa," Amber said, attempting to brighten the mood. "Just in time for my graduation."

"Well, at least Mom will."

"What about you?"

"You may as well know this. I'm going to find a way to stay. I belong there. And Amber, this time I'm not coming back."

Ted Barlow came into Heather's room waving a packet. "Guess what I picked up from our travel agent today."

"Our tickets? Oh, Dad, let me see." Heather snatched the packet from his hand and opened it. "Yes!" she said. "Here they are." She waved the tickets high in the air, then hugged her father.

Amber watched from her perch atop the desk chair in Heather's room, her heart sinking. It was really going to happen. Heather and their mother were going off to Africa in a week. Amber and their dad would remain behind.

"You'll land at Gatwick in London, spend the day sightseeing, then board a British Air flight for Entebbe," he said. "The trip takes two full nights of flying. I hope you're up to it."

"I did it at Christmas, remember?"

"Then I hope Janet's up to it." He appraised Heather through narrowed eyes. "You look a bit thin to me. You eating right?"

"I'm not very hungry these days—too excited." Heather stuffed the tickets back into the packet and plopped it beside Amber on the desk. "See—I'm packing."

A large suitcase lay open in one corner. Casual clothing, shoes, and other personal items lay in neat, organized rows across the floor.

"You've been packing for days," Amber grumbled. "How long can it take?"

"Don't you have homework?" Ted asked.

Amber bristled. "No."

"Did you finish the application forms for the University of Miami you brought home last week?"

"Almost."

"How long can it take to fill out a simple form? Amber, please get serious about this. The freshman class will close out and you won't get in."

"Wouldn't that be a tragedy?" she muttered.

Heather stepped between them. "You two have got to learn to get along better. Neither Mom nor I will be here to referee."

"Referee what?" Janet stepped into Heather's room. She kissed her husband and he slid his arm around her.

"The dynamic duo." Heather inclined her head toward Amber and their father.

"We're going to be fine," Ted said, leveling a look at Amber that dared her to disagree.

"I hope so," Janet said. "I received my itinerary from the FACES organization today, and I've got quite a surgical schedule facing me. First we go to the hospital in Lwereo for two weeks."

"Alice will be Mom's first patient," Heather said, waving a letter. "Paul and Jodene are thrilled. You're going to love them, Mom."

"I'm sure. But afterward I head to Kampala, where I'll have four weeks straight of nonstop surgery. Not only will I have local residents, but they're bussing in refugees from Rwanda and Sudan as well. Lots of children with deformities, but also plenty with war injuries. I hope I'm up to the task."

Ted gave her shoulders a squeeze. "You're up to it."

"I wish you were going with me."

"Next time."

Amber's stomach tightened. Not once had anyone in her family glanced her way as they made their plans. She was invisible.

"I'm staying with Paul and Jodene the whole time," Heather said.

"I'd rather we weren't separated," Janet said, "but you really are better off at the Children's Home. By the end of each day I'll be ready to drop, so I really won't be fit company for you."

"I'll have plenty to do in Lwereo, believe me. Boyce will keep me company."

Amber listened to Heather and her mother make plans, heard her father interject a comment now and again. They never once looked at her, never once asked her a question. She was Amber, the Nonexistent One. Without a word she slipped from the room, and no one seemed to notice.

An unfamiliar sound awakened Amber in the middle of the night. She pulled her pillow over her head, but the noise intruded. She sat up, listened. It sounded as if someone was being sick in the bathroom. From beneath the bathroom door that adjoined her and Heather's bedrooms, Amber saw a fine line of light breaking the darkness in her room. She threw off her covers and padded to the door.

She knocked softly. "Sis? Is that you?"

No answer, only the sound of retching.

Amber knocked a second time. "Heather, are you okay?"

The sound stopped, but the quiet sent an ominous chill up Amber's spine. She twisted the doorknob and eased the door open. She blinked in the glaring light and stifled a scream. On the floor, Heather lay unconscious, her blood staining the toilet bowl and the pristine white tiles like a ring of bright red fire.

6

Amber had been around hospitals all her
life, but she had never been so unprepared as she was in the emergency room that
night waiting to hear word of her sister. Hours
before, when she'd discovered Heather on the
bathroom floor, she'd run yelling into their
parents' room. She'd awakened them, followed
them back down the hall, listened to them as
they worked on Heather, bouncing between
the roles of terrified parents and seasoned
medical professionals. An ambulance had been
called, and Heather, still unconscious, had been
whisked away.

"Stay here!" Ted Barlow had barked as he
and Janet climbed into the ambulance with
Heather and the paramedics.

"No way," Amber had muttered beneath her

breath as the ambulance screeched out of the circular driveway. She had hopped into her car and followed the screaming ambulance through the late-night streets to the sprawling Jackson Memorial Hospital complex, where she now paced, frightened and trembling, across the floor of the emergency room waiting area.

The wall clock told her it was three A.M., but based on the number of people waiting to be treated, it could have been the middle of the afternoon. Old people, young people, sick people, and some who looked perfectly well sat in rows of chairs, talking, crying, drinking endless cups of coffee bought from a vending machine. The admittance desk had a line of people waiting to be processed. At the end of the hall stood the doors to the triage area, which had swallowed up Amber's family hours before.

Amber had begged a busy nurse to tell her parents she was in the waiting room, but she had no way of knowing if they'd gotten the message. She figured her father would be angry with her for coming, but she didn't care. Surely he must realize that Amber couldn't have sat at home waiting for the phone to ring. Surely her mom had to know how scared Amber must be. Once again she felt invisible, as if her feelings and concerns didn't count for anything with her parents.

She had almost screwed up her courage to barge through the triage doors when she saw her father coming toward her, looking worried and exhausted. She rushed to meet him. "How's Heather? What happened to her?"

"We got the bleeding stopped, but we still don't know what's caused it. She's going upstairs into Internal Medicine's ICU, and we'll begin more extensive tests tomorrow."

"Sh-She's not coming home?"

"She's taken a unit of whole blood since we've been here. She can't go home until we get to the bottom of this."

"Where's Mom?"

"Upstairs with Heather."

"Can I see Heather?"

Ted raked a hand through his already disheveled hair. "I came to take you to her."

They hurried to the elevator and rode up in silence. Amber shivered, more from tension and fear than from cold. "Are you mad at me for coming?" she asked.

He shook his head. "I know you're worried too."

"I am, Daddy. I really am. Th-There was so much blood. . . ." Her voice broke and she began to cry.

Her father put his arms around her and held her. "I'm mad at myself," he said against her hair. "I should have had her in for a thorough physical exam when she returned from Africa."

Amber lifted her head. "You think going to Africa made her sick?"

"I don't know. It's possible, though."

Amber's mind spun at the implication. Heather had lived half her life with the dream of going to Africa. How cruel it would be if the fulfillment of her dream was the source of her illness. "Maybe it's just the flu or something," she mumbled.

The elevator stopped and the doors slid open.

"Maybe," her father echoed.

They walked down the dimly lit hall hand in hand, his grip telling Amber that he didn't believe for a minute that Heather had a complicated case of the flu. Amber didn't believe it either, but it was the only straw of hope she had to grasp at.

*   *   *

Three days later, after a battery of tests and no definitive answers, Heather was released from the hospital and sent home. She was restricted to bed rest and a bland diet, neither of which she welcomed. "I don't feel like staying in bed," she told her mother. "And I don't want anything to eat."

"Since when are your doctor's orders up for debate?" Janet asked, fluffing the bed pillows.

"But I feel fine."

Amber, who was busy sorting through a stack of videos she'd rented for Heather to watch, listened but kept her opinions to herself. Heather's mysterious malady had given all of them a real scare, and to Amber's way of thinking, it seemed as if Heather's doctors had let them down by not discovering the source of her abdominal pain and bleeding. Their parents were frustrated and baffled as well, but without a diagnosis, they could do nothing more than keep a close watch on Heather. Amber knew that Heather still had pain because she sometimes saw Heather grimace. And despite Dolores's secret recipe for delicious chicken soup, Heather still wasn't eating properly.

Janet put her hands on her hips and in a no-nonsense voice said, "You will stay in bed, young lady, until you return for a checkup at the end of the week. *If* your doctor gives you permission to resume regular activities at that time, *then* you may. End of discussion. Now, I've got to return to my office; I have a consultation at five. If you need anything, ring for Dolores. Or ask Amber. Once school's out for the day, she'll be your personal slave. Right, Amber?"

Amber curtsied. "Just snap your fingers and I'll do your bidding, Cinderella."

Heather made a face. "I don't want to be waited on. I've still got things to do before we leave next week."

Janet's eyes narrowed. "You're not going anywhere."

"But the trip—"

"Is out. Don't argue," Janet added firmly when Heather opened her mouth. "Even if you were well, which you aren't, your immune system is weakened. Africa is no place for someone who isn't one hundred percent physically healthy. I shouldn't have to tell you that."

Amber came over to the bed, reading the shock and disappointment in Heather's face. "How about you, Mom? Will you go?"

"I've got a call in to the FACES head-quarters to explain that I'm dropping out. They'll understand."

"But people are counting on you!" Heather cried. "You can't cancel. Don't you under-stand? You're the hope for a normal life for Alice, for lots of children over there. You have to go!"

"I have to stay home and take care of my daughter," Janet answered calmly.

"But I have doctors to take care of me. Isn't that so?" Heather protested. "And Dad will be here. He won't let anything happen to me. Please go."

"I don't want to go alone. I only agreed to go in the first place because you wanted it so much. I was going because of you, Heather. And because I could do some good, but *you* were the impetus to get me to Uganda."

"But you gave your word. Jodene and Paul are expecting us."

Heather began to cry, and Amber shot their mother an anguished look.

"No one expects a mother to go off and leave her sick child," Janet said, attempting to soothe Heather. "Others will go. Someone will fill in for me. You'll see."

"But we already have our airplane tickets—expensive tickets. Are you going to just throw them away?"

"The money is the least of my concerns. I don't like backing out either, honey, but you are my first priority. What kind of a help would I be if I was thinking about you day and night? Listen, I'll make a deal with you. You get well and get your doctor's okay, and we'll go later."

"But Alice can't wait. She needs her surgery now—before she learns to talk. You know kids with cleft palates have serious speech problems. You're sentencing her to a lifetime of ridicule."

"That's not fair, Heather. Don't lay a guilt trip on me because I'm choosing you over a needy baby."

"I'll go in Heather's place." Heather and Janet swiveled toward Amber. She lifted her chin and repeated her statement.

"That's impossible." Janet waved her hand in dismissal.

"Wait," Heather said, leaning forward. "Hear her out, Mom."

Amber took a breath. "I know what you're going to say, Mom. 'You have school.' Well, I only have about six weeks of classes left, and everyone knows we seniors are just marking time in our final days. As for my grades, they're passable. B's in everything except chemistry, and that's a high C. What if I talk to each of my teachers and get their permission to take my finals early? If they say yes, that should take care of your and Dad's objection about school, shouldn't it?"

"Amber, it's your senior year. You're getting ready to graduate. You'll miss out on all the fun."

"What fun? Toilet-papering the campus for our senior prank? Having the principal threatening to hold back our diplomas until the culprits confess? I don't mind missing that."

"Your offer's generous," Janet said with a shake of her head. "But I still can't go halfway around the world while Heather's in a medical crisis."

"I accept Amber's offer," Heather blurted out. "It's the next best thing to going myself. And I'll be a lot more agreeable, a lot more cooperative, if I know the two of you are going ahead with our plans."

"I don't know. . . . Your father—"

"Think about it," Heather urged. "Send Dad to talk to me. He'll agree."

Amber stepped back, her heart hammering. Heather was doing the job of persuasion without her help, and she thought it best to leave it that way. Her offer had been genuine, and while she wasn't all that crazy about hanging out in Africa for six weeks, she'd do anything to help her sister. She was finished with high school anyway. Just that morning she'd learned that Dylan had asked Jeannie to the prom. Not that Amber had wanted to go with him after the way he'd been treating her. However, she knew that going to Africa would not only make Heather happy, it would also release her from the social shame of being unceremoniously dumped by her longtime boyfriend. Amber gave her sister an encouraging smile, knowing that while she might not be able to save the world, at least, for the time being, she could save herself.

It was Ted Barlow who came up with the solution for his wife to be in constant communication with him and Heather. "A special technically advanced satellite system phone," he said at the next evening's family meeting, held in Heather's room. "How do you think journalists and disaster relief workers communicate when they disappear into parts of the world without normal means of communication? International wireless cell phones use low-Earth-orbit satellites to send and receive signals. We'll get one for you, honey. No need for you to be cut off from us. You can call anytime to check on Heather, plus we can call you, too."

"But what if I'm in surgery when you call and I don't hear the phone ring?"

"We can get you an international pager if that will make you feel more comfortable. I'll leave you a voice mail, and you can pick it up whenever you're back to the phone."

"Mom, it sounds like the answer to my prayers," Heather said. "You can keep your word to FACES *and* stay in touch. We can talk every night if you want. I mean, after you take into account the seven-hour time difference."

"The FACES organization did sound disappointed when I called them," Janet said. "They said the hospitals where I was being sent were already taking applications for surgeries. Plus other doctors were coming to observe."

"Doesn't sound as if backing out is going to be easy," Ted said.

"Don't let them down, Mom," Heather pleaded. "I'll be the best patient in the world while you're gone. And I'll get well, too. I promise."

Amber sensed that her mother was wavering, so she cleared her throat and stepped forward. "I got a verbal okay from every one of my teachers." She didn't mention that her chemistry teacher had insisted she turn in a theory paper before she left. Or that her English teacher had demanded a ten-page report on Chaucer.

"Now, hold on," her father said. "I'm not in favor of *you* going. But there's no reason for your mother to back out. We both know the difficulties in picking up a qualified surgeon at the last minute. So, with her commitment made and the phone problem covered, I believe she should go. As for you—"

"But I want to go," Amber said, knowing that this had to be the most persuasive speech she had ever made. "I can help do the work Heather had agreed to do. And I can keep Mom company." She looked her father in the eye. "I could tell you that it's a great educational opportunity for me, but you probably wouldn't buy it. I could promise that I'll be perfect and not cause any problems, but you wouldn't believe that, either. But, Dad, Mom, I want this more than anything I've wanted in a long, long time. I want to go with Mom to Uganda. Say yes, Dad. I'm begging you—will you *please* let me go in Heather's place?"

7

It wasn't until Amber was well over the Atlantic Ocean ten days later that she could take a deep breath and relax. She considered all that she'd had to accomplish to accompany her mother to Uganda. In school she'd finished two papers and six exams in five days and three all-nighters. She'd passed everything, not much caring about the grades, only wanting to leave the high-school scene far behind.

She'd gotten the immunizations necessary for travel to Africa, told her friends she'd see them at graduation, and pointedly ignored Dylan. She'd heard through the grapevine that he and Jeannie had been at each other's throats and that he was avoiding the girl. Amber couldn't say she was sorry to hear the news.

With school behind her, she'd spent two

days shopping, then packing under Heather's watchful and often teary gaze.

"I'd give anything in the world to be going," Heather had said.

"You just concentrate on getting well. Who knows? If your checkup goes okay, maybe you can talk Dad into flying you over to join us."

"Maybe."

But Amber didn't believe that would happen. Heather still had terrible abdominal cramps, and although her doctor had switched her medication twice, she had difficulty keeping food down.

Amber had listened to everything her sister told her about Africa—which was plenty. She learned names and faces from photographs of the people Heather cared about, the kinds of food to avoid, the way Africans kept time ("They don't. They just show up whenever they feel like it.") and, by poring over a map, learned the various regions Heather thought she might enjoy visiting. Amber had taken notes and made silent promises to herself never to venture any farther than she had to. She wasn't the least bit excited about facing outdoor bathrooms and rainwater showers, but she'd never let on to her sister.

"I'll be your eyes and ears," she'd promised the night before leaving.

"Better yet, be my heart," Heather had told her.

Amber and her mother had boarded a five P.M. flight to London, settled into their first-class seats, and buckled their seat belts. Amber's last image of home had been the city of Miami spread out like colorful confetti along a shoreline of glittering green water as the plane soared toward the clouds. Her last image of Heather had been of her holding their father's hand, sobbing and throwing them kisses from the gangway.

"I hope we're doing the right thing," Janet said now, half to herself, as the plane leveled off above the clouds.

"It's what Heather wants," Amber reminded her.

"You too, evidently. I've never seen you apply yourself with such determination in your life."

"I did it for Heather," Amber said. "Africa would never be my first choice for a vacation spot."

They landed in London, where the weather was cold and rainy, and spent an exhausting day sightseeing. Amber had toured the city with her parents the previous summer when they'd left Heather aboard the Mercy Ship. Then Amber had been terminally bored. Now the city seemed regal to her, like a stately old woman. Dark cabs and bright double-decker buses sputtered in jammed traffic. Busy Londoners huddled under their umbrellas as they hurried down streets lined with towering old houses. Gardens were just beginning to bloom, and trees wore the bright, lacy green of new spring.

They returned to the airport that night and caught the ten o'clock flight to Entebbe. After a second restless night of sleeping in their airline seats, they landed at eight the following morning on the runway of the only Ugandan airport large enough to accommodate a big jet. By then Amber's eyes felt gritty and her mind foggy. After clearing customs and exchanging currency, Janet negotiated a cab ride in a minivan into Kampala.

"The Hilton," she told the driver.

The air was warm but lacked Miami's soggy humidity. The sky was a vivid blue, the earth red and brown, spattered with bursts of green foliage. Cattle were being herded alongside the busy roadway by Ugandan women wearing colorful native dresses and balancing jugs of water and bundles of sticks on their heads. Their children tagged behind them like ducklings.

The smell of burning charcoal from cooking fires set up at endless small campsites saturated the air. Young girls held babies on their hips; small boys swatted flies with sticks and poked grazing cows into obedient circles. Groups of people walked briskly toward the city of Kampala, their bare feet sending up clouds of dust. Amber stared wide-eyed out the minivan's window, feeling more like a foreigner than she ever had in London. Now she was visiting a colorful and exotic world that she found fascinating.

This is the country my sister loves, she told herself. *I don't think I can.* She was greatly relieved to see the oasis surrounding the Hilton Hotel rise out of the heart of the city, an island of calm, quiet green. They exited the minivan, only to be accosted by a cluster of children asking for money. "Street trash! Go—leave these nice ladies alone!" the doorman barked, but before he could shoo them away, Janet gave each child an Ugandan dollar.

Inside, the hotel of stucco and glass was as modern as any in the United States, and Amber and her mother's spacious suite was cooled by welcome air-conditioning. Amber flopped across the bed and stretched luxuriously while Janet ordered room service.

"First I want a hot shower," Janet said. "Then we'll call home and let your father and Heather know we're here. Then we'll both take a nap. Paul Warring is meeting us in the lobby tomorrow morning at nine. Enjoy this bit of civilization, Amber, while you can. It's the last we'll see of it for a while."

Amber nodded and yawned. Her mother went into the bathroom, and soon Amber heard the shower. A kaleidoscope of images of home flashed in Amber's mind's eye, and suddenly she was engulfed by a wave of homesickness. She was halfway around the world, thousands of miles from all she had ever known. And she realized she was ill prepared.

Her skills—driving a car, navigating the mall, shopping for fashionable clothing, hanging out with her friends at the beach—counted for little in this exotic land where people set up housekeeping alongside the road, where cattle roamed the streets like privileged citizens and children darted from stranger to stranger begging for enough money to feed themselves.

Amber's mother woke her at seven the next morning. "Let's get a move on," Janet said. Amber moaned but obeyed. By nine they had their gear packed and were in the lobby, where a brown-haired man in his early thirties introduced himself as Paul Warring.

"You look like your sister," he told Amber. "Jodene and I are sorry Heather couldn't come. She's an extraordinary young woman."

As they chatted, Paul loaded their things into a minivan. An Ugandan driver, introduced as Patrick, smiled his welcome. "I met your sister on the ship," Patrick said. "She is a one-and-only person."

"Heather told me about you," Amber replied. "She said you and Ian were good friends."

"Yes. . . . So sad about Ian. But he is with God now. A better place to be, I think."

Amber refrained from saying that Ian's leaving had brought Heather immeasurable heartache and that she personally wished God had not taken Ian away.

"Patrick's studying for the pastorate," Paul said. "Ugandan ministers are in great demand within the country."

"And when you write your sister, please tell her that I have found the girl of my dreams and that I'm engaged. Tell her I plan to be the husband of only one wife for all my life," Patrick said with a laugh.

Heather had told Amber about the Ugandan custom of polygamy. It had spread the AIDS epidemic through the population as well as causing many other problems. "I'll tell Heather. She'll be very happy for you both."

"She is invited to the wedding in September. Perhaps her illness will have passed by then."

"Hope so," Amber said, wondering again if Heather's health problem had been caused by something she'd picked up in Africa.

Paul and Janet spoke about Alice, and Amber listened, all the while watching the countryside bump past. The road was poor, covered with potholes that often forced the van to a crawl. They stopped once to buy the finger-sized bananas Heather had called "delectable." The vendor's small wooden cart stood at the side of the road next to a sign declaring that the area was on the equator. Paul snapped a photo of Amber and Janet beside the sign.

Hours later they entered the compound of the Kasana Children's Home, where Paul's family emerged from a brick house. After introductions, Jodene showed them to the small guest house. Amber chose the same room and bed where Heather had told her she'd stayed. She imagined Heather in every corner of the room. And while Amber didn't share Heather's attraction to Africa, she found it oddly comforting and less lonely to be in the same space that her sister had occupied.

Janet dumped her luggage and insisted on going straight to the hospital to check out the facility where she would operate on Alice. "I'd like you to bring Alice over this afternoon," she told Jodene. "I want to give her a thorough physical exam so that I can map out a surgical strategy."

With her mother gone, Amber was left to explore the grounds. She freshened up and set off, looking for the spots Heather had described so vividly. She found the pavilion where church suppers were held, and the outdoor kitchen, whose oven was being tended by several kids baking bread. They smiled and waved. She found the tree where Heather used to sit and wait for Kia. She turned when she heard the front door of the house slam. A little girl ran toward her, her face lit with a smile. She skidded to a stop in front of Amber, her smile exchanged for a look of puzzlement.

Amber bent and extended her hand. "I'll bet you're Kia."

The child nodded.

"Did you think I was Heather?"

Another nod.

"I'm Amber; Heather's my sister. You know, my *dada*." Amber used the Swahili word for "sister," which Heather had taught her. "Heather couldn't come, so I came for her. She gave me this to give to you." Amber reached into the pocket of her pink shorts and pulled out a piece of hard candy.

Shyly Kia took the candy and unwrapped it. "Thank you, Amber."

The girl's sweet smile touched Amber, and she understood how Heather had fallen in love with her. "Heather told me a lot about you. I hope we can be friends too."

The soft air hung around them like folds of a blanket.

"Heather!" a male voice shouted.

Amber turned to see a guy trotting toward her. He wore khaki shorts and construction boots and was bare from the waist up. His body was streaked with dirt and sweat. A red bandanna held reddish brown hair off his forehead. His smile reminded her of the sunlight. He was, in her quick evaluation, the best-looking creature she'd ever laid eyes on.

8

A mber straightened. The bare-chested young man skidded to a stop in front of her, a look of confusion clouding his face. "I'm sorry—I thought you were someone else," he said with a heavy Southern accent.

She grinned. "I'm Amber. I'll bet you're Boyce Callahan."

"Guilty. How'd you know?"

"Heather showed me pictures."

"I knew you'd be coming in her place, but when I saw you from a distance—well, you looked so much like her that I thought somehow she was well and had come instead."

He looked disappointed, and Amber felt a twinge of jealousy. No guy had ever seemed as eager to see Amber, and Boyce and Heather were just friends. At least, that was what Amber had thought. "No, she's still under her doctor's care. And we really don't look that much alike . . . do we?"

He grinned, and his green eyes crinkled at the corners. "It's sort of like looking at two roses. Same flower, just different styles."

Flattered, not knowing how to respond, she looked down at Kia. "I—um—was just getting to know Kia. My mom went to the hospital to take a look around. I'm sure you know she's going to—" Amber interrupted herself, afraid to say too much in front of the little girl. "Well, you know," she finished lamely.

Boyce crouched and gave Kia a grin. "What've you got there?"

Kia held out the candy, now grown sticky in her hand. "From Heather," she said with an adoring look at Boyce. "Heather's *dada*," she added, pointing at Amber.

"Heather sent you a present too," Amber told Boyce.

He stood. "She did?"

He looked like an eager puppy. "It's back in my quarters," Amber said with a laugh.

"I'm taking a lunch break. Could I get it now?"

"What do you say, Kia? Should we go get his present?"

Kia slipped her hand into Boyce's, and the three of them returned to the guest house. Inside, Amber rooted through her duffel bag and pulled out a jar of peanut butter.

"All right!" Boyce said.

"She told me how much you liked the stuff."

"Good timing. My supply's getting low." He opened the top and scooped a large dollop onto his finger. It was halfway to his mouth when he stopped himself. "Oh, sorry. Want some?" He tipped the open jar toward her.

"I'll pass this time."

He sucked the goo off his finger and replaced the lid. "Nectar of the gods," he said. "Thanks for hauling it all the way from the States. You made my day."

"Gee, it took so little. What do you do around here for fun?"

"Why don't I come by later and take you around and *show* you what we do for fun?"

Her heart skipped a beat. "It just so happens that my evening is free."

He set a time, then took Kia's hand again. Amber stood on the porch, watching them walk away, and told herself that so far Africa was turning out to be a really interesting place. She'd not been in the country two days and already she had a date with a gorgeous guy. "Not bad," she said under her breath. "Not bad at all."

She and her mother went to dinner that evening at Jodene and Paul's, where the table was filled with platters of vegetables fresh from the garden, home-baked bread, and a roasted chicken. Amber thought about Heather back home, unable to eat.

"What's your opinion of Alice?" Paul asked Amber's mother. "What are her chances for a successful surgery?"

"I assessed her thoroughly today. Sometimes there's a host of other problems that go along with the clefting. Fortunately, Alice's case isn't the worst type of this defect. It's operable. The actual surgery is done in two steps. I'll fix the palate first. That takes around an hour, with a five-day recovery time. Then the lip will be repaired next week and her nostrils brought into a more normal alignment. Dr. Gallagher and I both think she's an ideal candidate for the surgery."

"Will she have a scar?" Jodene asked.

"Yes, until she's a bit older; eventually it will begin to fade. More surgery when she's older will enhance her face cosmetically, but that will have to be evaluated by another surgeon. She's been well cared for, thanks to you two, and that's in her favor also."

"Believe me, it was a group effort," Jodene said. "I couldn't have done it without the help of all the young women who live on the premises. Everyone pitched in. We want her to have as normal a life as possible, and her physical appearance is an important part of the quality of her life. Thank you for taking time out of your busy life to come all the way to help Alice and kids like her."

"Heather sent me," Janet said with a smile. "She can be very persuasive."

"We know that," Paul said with a laugh. "But regardless, we're grateful."

"When will you operate?" Jodene asked. "I want to prepare Kia for the separation from Alice."

"Tomorrow. Once I'm certain there aren't any complications, I'll head back to Kampala." Janet looked directly at Amber. "And my thanks to you for letting Amber stay with you while I work in the city. I'm taking her to the hospital tomorrow, and Dr. Gallagher will assign her some work. If there's anything you need her to be doing, just let her know."

"We're delighted to have her," Jodene said smoothly. "Any sister of Heather's is welcome."

They laughed, but Amber was steamed. Her mother made it sound as if Amber couldn't be trusted to be productive on her own.

After dinner Boyce stopped by the house, met Janet, and invited Amber for a walk around the compound. Once outside, Amber blew out a sigh of relief. "Thanks for the rescue," she said. "My mom and I've spent entirely too much time together these past few days."

"That's me—Sir Boyce the Lionhearted." Dusk was falling, and the sky's brilliant shade of red orange had faded to a dusky purple. "Come take a look-see at the irrigation project while there's still enough light." Boyce took her hand and started up a trail through the bush.

They emerged into a clearing where trenches were being dug in a pattern. "Irrigation canals," Boyce explained. "My idea is to shuttle water down them to the sides of fields where crops can be planted. The water will come from this concrete reservoir—it'll collect rainwater. We're also digging a well to an underground lake. In a year or two this whole area will be green and fertile."

Amber gazed out over the parched ground, cracked from the blazing sun. "It's hard to imagine," she said. "But I believe you'll do it."

"It'll take most of three months to get it going. Paul will take over when I have to leave. If I don't finish up at Alabama by the end of next year, my daddy's going to write me off."

"How could he? You're doing so much good."

"Dad wants me working in his engineering firm. Personally, I'd rather put in a few years over here before settling down stateside. Africa gets in a person's blood, you know."

"Yes, it happened to Heather."

"But not to you?"

She didn't want to tell him how much the lifestyle *didn't* appeal to her, so she just shrugged and said, "I've only been here two days. Maybe in time."

"And here I am dragging you around when you'd probably rather be catching some Z's."

"I can sleep in tomorrow," she said. "Show me more."

The moon began to rise over a clump of trees and cast the land in a cool, pale light. Amber wished she was with Boyce back in Miami, where she knew of many places they could go to be together. She'd love showing him off to her friends. To Dylan, too.

Boyce took her to an area on the grounds with large thatched-roof buildings of cinder block. "These are the family units. I'll take you to Patrick's."

They found Patrick leading his group in a Bible study. "Come in! Come in," he told Boyce and Amber. "We are almost finished."

The main room held a mixture of hand-carved and secondhand furniture. Short hallways branched out from the larger room, separating the boys' and girls' sleeping quarters. The concrete floor was covered with a woven grass rug. Shields and masks hung on one wall; a painting of Jesus praying in the Garden of Gethsemane hung on another. When Patrick saw Amber staring at the shields, he said, "This reminds us of our heritage." He nodded toward the painting. "This reminds us of our hope. 'He who lives by the sword, dies by the sword,' " he quoted. " 'But the Word of the Lord stands forever.' "

Unable to think of anything to say, Amber smiled politely.

"Be right back," Boyce said. "I need to talk to one of my foremen."

Amber stood, feeling self-conscious and out of place. The group of Africans stared at her, some smiling, some whispering. "Meet my fiancée," Patrick said. "This is Ruth Musembe, soon to be Mrs. Patrick Sugabi."

Ruth, a diminutive young woman with a pleasant smile and wide-set features, didn't look much older than Amber. "Congratulations," Amber told her.

"I remember your sister," Ruth said. "She was so very brave to bring Alice out of Sudan. A dangerous place for both of them."

"That's my sister. Trying to save the world."

Patrick went to talk to Boyce, and Amber found herself alone with Ruth, forced to make small talk. "So where's your family?"

"In Rwanda. My parents are missionaries serving in my uncle's village, doing the work of the Lord."

"I'll bet they're looking forward to your wedding."

"Yes. It is an honor for me to marry Patrick." Ruth cut her eyes toward her fiancé, and her expression turned wistful, almost sad. "I pray each day to the Lord Jesus that I will be a good wife."

"I'm sure you will be." Amber thought Ruth far too serious for one who was soon to become a bride. She wore no engagement ring. Neither had she talked about a honeymoon, or buying things for herself or a new house. "Will you live here?"

"For a time, yes. Then we will become missionaries and move out into the bush to spread the Gospel."

Amber realized she didn't have much in common with this girl. Becoming an itinerant preacher's wife before she was twenty and living off the land didn't sound very appealing to her, but she hoped she seemed more enthusiastic about it than she felt. She didn't want to hurt Ruth's feelings.

When it was time for Amber and Boyce to leave, Ruth said, "It is pleasant to know you. You are like your sister in some ways, but you are yourself, too."

On the walk to the guest house in the moonlight, Amber asked, "Everybody loved Heather, didn't they?"

"Yes," Boyce said.

"You too?"

"She's my sister in the Lord. I love her like a sister. Believe me, Amber, a lot of workers come through the Mercy Ship program, and most are dedicated. But few have the intensity, the heart, the sheer love for mankind that Heather has. God used her in a mighty way while she was here. Perhaps he will use her again. I don't know. I do know that I count it a privilege to know her." He stopped at the doorway of the guest house. "You've come as her emissary, and I think that's admirable too."

Her heartbeat quickened. "We're different," she said. She didn't want him to think she was her sister's clone. "We don't exactly think the same way."

"Maybe not as different as you think. Wait until you've been challenged. Then you'll see what I mean."

He told her good night, and she went inside. Her mother was asleep, so she got ready for bed quietly and slipped under the clean sheets. She lay in bed, staring at the moon through the screen of the bedroom window, her mind jumbled with thoughts.

It dawned on Amber that Heather had truly achieved a kind of cult status at the compound. Amber's motives for coming hadn't been pure—she had wanted a change of scenery, a way to perk up her boring life. Coming to Africa on Heather's behalf seemed logical and altruistic. But it had also been self-serving. She felt like a fish out of water among these gentle people dedicated to serving God. How long before one of them discovered that she was a fraud?

9

Amber's plan to sleep in changed quickly when her mother routed her out of bed early the next morning. "We have to be at the hospital in an hour," Janet said. "This isn't a vacation, you know."

Although her mother's bossiness irritated Amber, she refrained from complaining. After all, Heather had kept such a schedule, and so could she.

At the hospital her mother went off to perform surgical duties, and Dr. Gallagher assigned Amber to the Women's Clinic, an outpatient operation that handled routine immunizations, performed TB testing, and dispensed information about birth control and HIV. Local women were lined up with their children from the minute the doors opened. An Ugandan nurse named Grace explained the counseling process to Amber, and to Amber's great surprise, she was left on her own to counsel native women about the various forms of birth control.

She felt overwhelmed at first, and embarrassed to be talking about such things with strangers. The women seemed incredibly young, and most had two or three children clustered around their chairs. But they looked eager to learn what she had to say, and before she knew it the morning had flown and Grace was excusing her to go to lunch. She stepped out the door and ran into Ruth.

"I didn't know you worked here," Amber said, pleased to see a familiar face.

"I do counseling in another room."

"What do you tell the women? Saying the same things about birth control all day long sure gets old. Maybe you can help me do a better job. Maybe we should work together. That would be good, don't you think?"

"I counsel women with other problems." Ruth looked uneasy, as if Amber's suggestion had upset her.

An awkward moment of silence passed. Finally, noticing that Ruth's hair was covered by a white cloth and her dress by a white apron, Amber asked, "Are you a nurse? You look so professional."

"I am an apprentice. When Patrick and I are serving in the bush, I will have to care for villagers. I am learning how."

"Can we eat lunch together?" Amber changed the subject when her stomach rumbled.

"Thank you, but I do not have time."

"So where's the cafeteria?"

Ruth gave Amber a blank stare.

"You know, the place where the staff go to eat their meals."

Ruth shook her head. "You must bring food with you. Only the patients are fed at the hospital."

Embarrassed by her *faux pas*, Amber shrugged. "Silly me. I forgot to bring anything. Oh, well . . . I'll skip lunch. Besides, it's almost time for Alice's surgery, and I'd planned to hang around until it's over. Can you please tell Grace what's going on? Tell her I'll be here in the morning, though. I don't want her to think I've deserted her." She realized she was babbling. "Got to run. Catch you later."

Amber took off toward the surgical wing, made a wrong turn, and found herself in an unfamiliar ward filled with male patients.

Every bed was occupied, and more patients had been placed on mats lining the floor. A man in a makeshift traction device consisting of wooden rods, pulleys, and rope, called out to her in Swahili. *"Maji. Tafadhali, maji."*

"I—I don't understand."

The man in the bed next to him said, "He wants water, please."

"I—I'll get a nurse." Amber looked around for someone—anyone. The room held only the sick and hurt. There were no nurses or orderlies.

"You are a nurse," the man said.

"No. I—I'm only a helper."

"Maji, maji," another called.

All at once other patients began to cry out to her, some in pain, some in anger. One man on the floor grabbed for her foot, making her squeal. Panicked, she said, "I'll send someone." She backed out of the ward, turned, and ran toward an outside door with the men's cries chasing her.

"Mom, I'm not cut out for this."

An hour later Amber stood in the area directly outside the operating room with her mother, sniffling back tears and telling her mother what had happened. Janet was dressed in pale green scrubs, preparing for Alice's surgery.

Janet shook her head. "Listen to me, Amber, you can't fall apart. I don't have time for it. I know things are hectic—"

"Things are *bizarre*," Amber corrected. "Sick people are lying on floors, the equipment is dilapidated, there's not enough of anything to go around—"

Janet took hold of Amber's shoulders. "Stop it. I know conditions are primitive by our standards, but this place is first-class compared to others I've seen. Now I have to go in there and operate on that baby. I have to concentrate and can't be worrying about you. So pull yourself together and wait for me. Jodene is coming over with Kia. Neither of them needs to see you in shambles." Janet let go of her daughter's arms. "You will be all right."

Chastised, Amber hung her head. "I—I'm sorry."

The operating room door opened and a nurse said, "We are ready, Dr. Barlow."

Janet tied her surgical mask over her mouth. "I've got to scrub. Can you manage?"

"I'm fine."

Her mother stepped inside the operating room. Amber glanced out the window and saw Jodene and Kia coming across the hospital's neatly trimmed grass. "How did you do this, Heather?" she asked under her breath. When Jodene and the child walked into the area, Amber put on a smile and announced, "You're just in time. Alice just went into surgery."

Jodene told Kia, "We'll visit Alice when the doctor is finished. Now we must wait."

"Does she understand what's happening?" Amber asked.

"I told her that Dr. Janet, the Mother Doctor of sisters Heather and Amber, is going to make Alice's face look like Kia's face. I think she gets it."

They sat on a hard wooden bench along the wall to wait. Unexpectedly, Kia handed Amber a small package wrapped in a banana leaf.

"What's this?" Amber took the green leaf and opened it. Inside lay two pieces of home-made bread.

"It's a peanut butter and honey sandwich," Jodene said. "Boyce and I thought you might be hungry. You know, it's not everyone he shares his peanut butter with," she added with a chuckle. "You must really be special."

The unexpected gesture of kindness touched Amber. "Thank you," she said to Kia. "I forgot to pack a lunch, and I'm really hungry."

The child's wide, trusting eyes tangled with Amber's gaze. "Mother Doctor will make my *dada* so that she can smile very pretty."

Emotion closed Amber's throat. "Yes," she said, suddenly proud of her mother's skills. She smoothed Kia's hair. "My mother can do that. She will make Alice's smile very pretty. Just like yours."

The surgery took an hour. Alice went to the recovery room, and Janet bent the rules and carried Kia there to see her sister. Jodene and Amber waited in the hall while Amber wondered if the sight of the surgical dressing would scare the child. But Kia returned looking satisfied, not frightened.

"I'm going to stay around for a while," Janet told Amber. "Why don't you go back to the house?"

"You're both having dinner with us," Jodene interjected. "Come straight over when you're finished."

"We've got to learn to fend for ourselves,"

Janet said. "You can't be feeding us every night."

"Nonsense. We like your company. And when you head off to Kampala at the end of next week, we expect Amber to eat all her meals with us."

For that Amber was grateful. Heather had had friends to eat with every night, but Amber would have no one once her mother left.

"Thanks," Janet said to Jodene. To Amber she said, "We'll call home tonight. I know your sister's sitting by the phone waiting for a full report."

Amber was certain her mother was correct.

After dinner Amber helped Jodene do dishes at a sink with a hand pump connected to an underground well, and Janet returned to the cottage to place the phone call. "Give me about twenty minutes to talk, then come," she told Amber.

Amber waited the allotted time, then hurried to the house to take her turn on the phone. "Hi, sis."

"Hi yourself. Mom says you've pitched right in at the hospital. It's different from medical care over here, isn't it?"

"I'll say. I feel sorry for the people. I'm counseling women about birth control," Amber added quickly. "Who'd have thought it?" Hurrying on, she said, "Patrick has a fiancée—Ruth."

"Patrick's engaged? That's wonderful! What's she like?"

"Sort of quiet. She and I don't have a lot in common, so it's not easy to have conversations with her. She's worrying about being a good missionary wife. She seems really nervous about it."

"Well, I'm sure if Patrick picked her out, she must be special. How's Boyce?"

"You didn't tell me he was so totally hunky."

"You saw photos of him."

"Grainy little snapshots," Amber corrected. "Up close and personal, he's pretty awesome."

"I'll write and tell him you said so."

"Don't you dare!" Amber squealed. "I'll never speak to you again if you do."

Heather laughed. "All right, I'll keep quiet. Now, tell me about everybody else. I want to hear what you think about everything."

Amber launched into a monologue about Alice and Kia, Jodene and Paul—anything she thought Heather might want to hear. Once she'd finished, she asked, "And how about you, sis? How are you doing?"

"I'm still having problems. The doctors are baffled, and Dad's on their backs all the time. I'm seeing another specialist on Friday. He's from Atlanta's CDC—Centers for Disease Control and Prevention."

"They think you're contagious?"

"No—but since they can't figure out what's wrong, they're trying everything. Maybe I did pick up something while I was in Africa." A chill went through Amber, but she didn't say anything. "I told Dad that hundreds of people travel to Africa and never catch anything, so if you're worried about it, stop worrying."

Amber blushed. Her sister knew her too well. "I'm not worried."

"I'm doing exactly what I'm told," Heather added. "Staying in bed, taking my medicine . . . Truth is, I don't feel much like doing anything else."

"Then do nothing! You can always shop QVC."

Heather laughed. "You nut! How's that shopping gene helping you in Uganda?"

"Give me time. I've only been here a few days."

"I miss you, Amber."

"I miss you, too." Amber swallowed the lump of emotion sticking in her throat and saw her mother signal her from the bedroom doorway. She told Heather, "Mom's giving me the evil eye. I'd better hang up."

"She said she'd call again after Alice's second surgery. Take care," Heather said, sounding teary. "And go easy on Boyce. He's already had his heart broken by Ingrid."

Amber hung up, thinking about everything Heather had said to her. She took the phone to her mother in the living room, asking, "What's your opinion of Heather's being seen by someone from CDC? What do you think he's looking for?"

"Your father's worried that she might have a mutant strain of the hepatitis virus."

"That's bad?"

"Yes," Janet said in her gravest tone. "That could be very bad indeed."

10

"I'm telling you, Boyce, it could be serious." Amber had sought out Boyce the next evening as soon as both had completed their work for the day. They had met under the pavilion because the sky was threatening rain.

"What exactly did your mother tell you?" Boyce asked. He was freshly showered, his hair still damp.

"She had some medical mumbo jumbo about the different strains of the hepatitis virus. It seems like science is constantly discovering some new strain of it—A, B, C . . . all the way up to G. The worst is C because it destroys a person's liver." Amber paced as she talked.

"Can't doctors give you an immunization shot against it? I got an armful of shots before I came here."

"Sure, for hepatitis A and B. But not C. And

according to Mom, there's no known treat-ment for it. What if Heather has hepatitis C? What if she begins to lose her liver function? A person can't live without a liver, Boyce."

Boyce took Amber's hand. "Slow down, girl. You're jumping to conclusions. What exactly did your mother tell you?"

"She said that a small percentage of the people who have it die from it."

"A *small percentage*," Boyce emphasized. "Be-sides, you don't know for sure that Heather even has the virus."

"That's why the doctor from CDC is com-ing to examine her. According to Mom, he's an old friend, someone they knew years ago when they were in the Peace Corps. He's some kind of specialist in infectious diseases. Not that Heather's contagious or anything. But what if she picked up this virus?"

"Then this guy will figure it out."

"Mom's going to call again before she heads off to Kampala. But she's taking the phone with her, so how will I find out anything?"

"If it's serious, she can reach Paul on his ham radio unit."

Amber chewed her bottom lip. "I'm worried

about her. Really worried. I don't want anything to happen to her."

"Heather's in good hands, and I'm sure her doctors will get to the bottom of her problem soon," Boyce said soothingly.

"I feel helpless. I wish there was something I could do for her."

"You can pray. Patrick and I meet every night for prayer. We'll put Heather at the top of our prayer list."

Amber didn't have as much confidence in prayer as Boyce did. "Do you really think God listens?"

"Yes. And because you come from a family of doctors, you should know that plenty of doctors also believe in the power of prayer. I read some studies scientists have done on the subject, and it's documented that people who pray, people who believe in God, recover more quickly and with a lot less stress. Even people who are prayed for without knowing that they're being prayed for recover faster."

"Really?" That sounded hopeful to Amber. If such a scientific study had been done, there had to be some truth to it. "I don't mean to sound skeptical," she said. "I—I just don't feel the same way about things that you do. About God and all."

Boyce looked her in the eye. "Faith is a gift from God, Amber. No one's born with it."

"I've never heard that before."

"Think about it. Our brains want everything spelled out for us. We want proof of something before we believe in it. Faith is trusting in what we can't see or touch. It's being changed from a person who must have things proved to a person who accepts the unprovable as true and real. That's a big leap for a lot of people. And one that only God can accomplish by faith."

Amber considered his explanation. Her sister had always been a person who wanted to help others. When the two of them were growing up, Heather had been the one who raised money for charity and organized food drives. But when she'd come home from Africa, she'd been different.

"Coming here, meeting up with you, Ian, Jodene, and Paul, changed Heather," Amber told Boyce. "Losing Ian was part of it; she was sad and she kept to herself more. But she was also more . . . focused. Quieter. It's hard to describe."

"She encountered a different world over

here. I know, because so have I. Being here changes your perspective on *our* world. Our American, sanitized, white-bread world," he elaborated. "Being changed isn't necessarily a bad thing, you know."

"Maybe, but to be honest, her change has bothered me. I've felt cut off from her. We're in the same house, but not in the same place. You know what I mean?"

"I think so."

"She said something happened to her spiritually. She and Dad had a discussion about it. I don't think any of us understand it, but it's real to Heather. She still wants to help people and all, but she wants to help them in a deeper way."

"Before God got to me, I was pretty wild," Boyce said. "In trouble at school, driving my parents crazy. But once God changed me, I felt like some fire was living inside me. I wanted to do something good with my life, something for others. Trouble was, no one believed I had changed. Coming to Africa was part of proving it. While I was on the Mercy Ship, I met a whole lot of people who felt the same way. Building something over here has made me feel useful. Like my life was counting for something. Not just for the sake of the orphans living here, but for God, too. Not that God needs any help from me," Boyce added with a laugh, "but it feels good to do something for him when he's done so much for me."

Rain had begun to fall, and the drops on the thatched roof made a muffled patter. Amber felt wrapped in a cocoon of softness and cut off from the march of time. "You sound like Heather," she said.

"I can't change who I am, Amber. I'm a man who loves God."

No guy had ever talked to Amber with such sincere, open honesty. It moved her. And it made her feel inadequate, as if she was missing a piece of something bigger. Back home, with her friends, with Dylan, she'd been able to feel as if she fit, as if pleasure and enjoyment were central to the scheme of life.

From Boyce and her work at the hospital she was discovering something outside herself, something independent and unimpressed by her presence. She stood at a doorway, but a doorway into *what* she did not know. Still, she had sense enough to realize that if she went through the door, she too would be changed.

And that was what made her feel uneasy. Once through it, there would be no turning back.

"I admire you for knowing who you are," she said above the patter of the rain. "I don't know that much about myself, although I wish I did. But I trust you. And if you're praying for Heather, I hope it will help her."

"Prayer is a way for us to talk to God, to ask him for something we want. Heather's in his hands. He'll watch over her."

And so was Ian, Amber thought, though she didn't say it. All the prayer in the world hadn't made a difference for him.

Alice's second surgery at the beginning of the next week went well, and once the dressings came off, everyone could see the dramatic improvement in her appearance. With Jodene and Kia, Amber visited the ward where Alice lay recovering. "It's the repair on the inside of her mouth and nasal cavity that's going to make the most difference in her life," Janet said when Jodene raved about her surgical skills. "Now she'll be able to learn to eat and talk properly."

"But it's the outside that people see," Jodene

reminded them. "Looking normal will really improve the quality of her life. You've worked wonders for her."

Janet waved aside the woman's praise. "By the time she's a toddler, the scar will be as thin as a pencil line." She smiled and smoothed the baby's hair. "Amber, take a few photos to mail off to your sister."

"I'll send along pictures as she improves," Jodene promised. "I know how much this little girl means to Heather."

"I'm turning her over to the nursing staff," Janet said, "and packing up for Kampala."

"Paul will take you whenever you're ready."

Once her mother left, Amber would be on her own, and although her work was going smoothly and she'd forged friendships with Jodene, Boyce, and a few others, this would be the first time in her life that she would be totally out of touch with her family. She thought back to the many times she'd wished they'd get out of her face—just disappear. Now that it was about to happen, she had mixed feelings.

Two days later, in the early hours of the morning, Janet prepared to leave. A call stateside the day before had revealed that the CDC specialist had been delayed in his trip to Miami, so nothing new had happened for Heather. "Don't work too hard," Heather had said cheerfully. But to Amber, her sister's voice didn't sound strong.

Paul loaded Janet's belongings, and Janet hugged Amber goodbye. "You going to be all right?"

"Jeez, Mom, I'm seventeen. I think I can handle a few weeks away from my mommy."

Janet sighed. "I was just asking."

Amber held herself rigid. "I'll be fine. When you talk to Heather, tell her I miss her. And Mom, if you find out anything about her health—"

"I'll get word to you," Janet said. She stepped into the van and leaned out the window. "Be good, okay?"

Amber rolled her eyes dramatically. "As if I could even find trouble around here."

"You have a knack, honey. . . ."

Paul started the engine and, as Janet waved to the small group gathered in the yard, pulled out. As the taillights disappeared, tears spilled from Amber's eyes. "I'm fine. I'm fine," she said, holding up her hand to ward off sympathy.

Boyce slung his arm over her shoulders. "Hey, it's Saturday. What would you say to taking the day off with me? We'll borrow the Jeep and I'll take you to one of the most beautiful places on planet Earth."

Boyce drove to the town of Kabale, in Uganda's mountainous region. "Lake Bunyoni, a crater lake six thousand miles above sea level," he told her as they took a winding, rough road cut through a thick jungle of towering trees and fallen branches. As the Jeep chugged upward, the air turned cooler, less humid and smothering. At the crest of the slope, the ground flattened and Amber looked out onto a breathtaking view of lush acres of mountain forests surrounding calm blue water. In the center of the lake she saw an island, and on it, a building that resembled a fortress. "What's that?"

"It's a school now, but once it was a leper colony built by the Dutch."

"Lepers! Like in the Bible?"

"We have a few cases in our hospital. The patients are housed in the back buildings, along with the AIDS and TB patients. But leprosy is treatable, even curable with modern drugs. We can paddle out to the island by canoe later if you want."

"I'll think about it," Amber said, shivering at the vision of people with open sores and rotting skin.

There was an inn at the top of the hill, accessible by steps carved out of the ground. A patio faced the lake. Boyce took Amber's hand. "Come on. I'll buy you lunch." They settled into chairs facing the lake, and Boyce ordered strong Ugandan coffee. Happy to get her mind off disease and sickness, Amber took a lungful of rain-scented air and listened to the exotic calls of wild birds and monkeys.

"This rain forest is the home of the only mountain gorillas in the world," Boyce told her. "They're shy animals that keep to themselves, and tourists come from all over the world on photo safaris to Bwindi National Park. Rangers protect the animals, but poachers still kill them."

"That's terrible."

"Sure is, especially when you consider there're only about six or seven hundred left."

"People certainly mess up the planet, don't they?" Amber sighed. "I'm glad you brought me here. It's really beautiful."

"I hoped you'd like it. When I'm up here, I feel like I'm on top of the world. Hard to believe that Rwanda is less than fifty kilometers away."

"Isn't that where some of Ruth's family is living?" Amber craned her neck in the direction Boyce pointed in, but all she could see were vast forests of trees.

"Yes. She once lived there too. Never again."

"What's wrong with Rwanda?"

"Civil war broke out in '90, and Ruth's village was burned to the ground."

"That's terrible. Was she hurt?"

Boyce furrowed his brow. "You mean you don't know?"

"Know what?"

"Her parents were away doing missionary work the night the rebels came and looted and burned her village. She was twelve years old and they dragged her off into the underbrush, raped her, and left her for dead."

11

Amber felt as if she'd been kicked in the stomach. "I—I didn't know. She's never said a word."

"That's why she counsels rape victims at the hospital. She knows what they're going through. She knows how violated they feel."

Amber had assumed that Ruth did the same type of counseling she did. Not counseling for rape victims. "Twelve . . . she was just a child."

"Right. But they didn't care. They were animals."

Amber shuddered. "She could have told me."

"I guess it's not something she talks about except to other rape victims. Besides, I think she's slightly in awe of you."

"Of me? Why?"

"You're Heather's sister. You're an American, and wealthy, and confident. Ruth's not had much contact with Westerners. She admires you."

Amber felt her cheeks color. "I'm the one who admires her. Especially now. I thought she didn't like me." All her life Amber had been shielded and protected, given good things and plenty of opportunities. In the light of Ruth's horrible trauma, Amber's life was a fairy tale. "Why did the rebels do such a terrible thing? Why destroy Ruth's village?"

"Because she was from the wrong tribe," Boyce explained. "Civil war is a fact of life in Africa. So is political unrest."

"Why didn't her parents leave Rwanda? I would think they'd never want to live there again."

"Staying took courage, all right. Plus, they're missionaries. It spoke volumes about forgiveness to villagers who had been attacked by the rebels. If Ruth's family had been home that night, they would have been murdered. But they weren't home. They believe God spared them to do good works, to spread the Gospel of love, not hate."

"How about Ruth? Why didn't God save *her*?"

"What makes you think God didn't save her?"

"But she was raped, and you said they were trying to kill her! What was she saved from?"

"What those men meant for Ruth's destruction, God used for her good. What happened to her was terrible, but it also sent her into Uganda. It put her with the Children's Home. It led her to Patrick and to their engagement."

"Well, I would think God might have figured out some other way to accomplish the same thing," Amber said indignantly.

Boyce toyed with the handle of his coffee cup. "God permits evil to exist, and he often uses evil to accomplish his purposes. God doesn't micromanage the universe, Amber. People have free will, and just because we don't get it doesn't mean it's not part of a bigger plan we can't see when we're going through something bad."

Boyce's notion that life worked out for the best regardless of the circumstances irritated Amber. "I still don't think it's fair. Ruth didn't deserve to have that happen to her."

"I agree. But it did happen to her. And because it happened, she's able to help others who've gone through the same thing. And don't you know? Life isn't fair." He tipped his head to one side and flashed her a mischievous smile. "If life *was* fair, I'd be able to get a stack of peanut butter and jelly sandwiches for lunch."

"Are you changing the subject?"

"Yes. But only because I brought you here to have a good time, not to make you mad at me."

"Fair enough," she said with a toss of her hair. She didn't like arguing with Boyce and didn't want their relationship to turn adversarial. "I'm hungry too. Maybe I'll be less crabby after lunch."

"You're not crabby," he said, signaling for the waiter. "You're curious. That's allowed. Ask questions whenever you want."

The waiter, a boy of about thirteen, hustled over and Boyce asked, "What's to eat?"

"Crayfish from the lake. Or chicken. Very good food. Very fresh." A grin split the boy's face.

Boyce opted for the crayfish; Amber chose the chicken.

"Below is the village," the boy said, pointing to a cluster of huts along the side of the lake. "I will gather a cook."

"It could be a long wait for lunch," Amber said, dismayed.

"Here, have some of these." Boyce opened a small backpack he'd laid by his feet and doled out two finger bananas and a pile of peanuts.

"I thought Uganda didn't have peanuts."

"They call them groundnuts." Boyce popped a handful into his mouth. "What they don't have is peanut *butter*. Instead they turn the nuts into a sauce to pour over meat. They also don't have bread, so I guess there's no reason for peanut butter to exist, is there?"

"Well, I've eaten *matoke*—Uganda's excuse for bread. It tastes like library paste."

"What's wrong with library paste? I ate a steady diet of it in second grade."

"I'll bet if we flavored it with peanut butter, you'd still eat it."

"Got any?"

Amber poked him in the side. "Don't make me slap you around," she joked.

They sat together in a long, comfortable silence, watching a woman walk up the hill. The boy who'd gone to get her was already back and stealthily tiptoeing up to a clump of bushes not far from the patio. He crouched and clucked softly. All at once a large rooster squawked and darted out from under a bush with the boy in hot pursuit. Amber began to laugh but stopped as the truth dawned on her. She grabbed Boyce's arm and straightened in her chair. "Uh—do you suppose that's my lunch?"

Boyce studied the drama unfolding below. "Probably."

"Yikes! Tell him to stop! I can't eat that poor thing!"

"Why? Where did you think they were going to find your chicken?"

"In a refrigerator."

Boyce laughed heartily. "There's no refrigeration up here. No stores, either. If you're hungry you pick it or catch it, then cook it and eat it."

Amber's stomach churned. "I think I'm going to be sick. Make him stop, Boyce. Tell him I've changed my mind."

Still laughing, Boyce called out to the boy in Swahili. The kid looked up, gave Amber a curious look, then shrugged and hiked up to the patio. The rooster stopped flapping and settled down to peck at bugs on the ground. "What would the lady like for lunch?" the boy asked. "The cook is waiting for the chicken."

By now the woman from the village was inside the building behind them, and Amber smelled the aroma of sautéing onions and tomatoes. Normally her mouth would have been watering in anticipation, but her appetite had fled. "Vegetables would be good," she said. "Just a plateful of cooked vegetables, please."

The boy exchanged looks with Boyce, who shrugged. "I still want the crayfish," he said. He handed the boy a few Ugandan dollars. "More coffee. I think the lady needs it."

She needed it, all right. She also needed a constant reminder of where she was: She was in a place where chicken didn't come in tidy little cellophane-wrapped packages. And wicked men thought nothing of taking a young girl by force simply because she belonged to a particular tribe. Simply because she was in the wrong place at the wrong time, with the wrong ancestors.

It was well past dark when Boyce and Amber returned to the mission compound. Jodene met them in the yard with an oil lamp. "The lake is beautiful, isn't it?" Jodene asked as Amber exited the Jeep.

"Gorgeous," Amber said. "But I think we hit every pothole in the road home. I wish I could soak in a hot bath."

"I know how you feel," Jodene said. "When we first arrived, we stayed with another missionary couple. They had a huge old Victorian tub—perfect for soaking. In fact, in the cities, many Ugandan homes have tubs left from the time the British ruled the country. Trouble is, the tubs have no plugs. The Ugandans threw them all away."

"How do they take a bath without a plug to stop up the drain?"

"No African would ever sit in dirty bathwater. They were appalled at the British custom. Instead, they fill a container with water, sit in an empty tub, and pour the water over themselves. All the dirty water goes down the open drain." Jodene shook her head, bemused. "Besides, water is precious during certain times of the year, and for one person to fill a tub and bathe when the same amount could water a field of crops, or some cattle . . . well, you can see how it appears wasteful to them."

Amber understood, but she still yearned for

a tub of hot water and scented bubbles. "I guess," she said with a sigh.

Boyce excused himself. "Church tomorrow," he said. "I'm speaking, and I want to see Patrick tonight."

"Speaking of Patrick, there's been some excitement," Jodene said. "Ruth received a message from her parents that her cousin Ann is also getting married. In fact, her father suggested that Ruth and Patrick come to Rwanda, to her uncle's village, and get married at the same time."

"Rwanda!" Boyce said.

After their conversation at the lake, Amber understood his alarm.

"Is she going?" he asked.

"They were waiting to talk to you. Ruth's scared, but she really wants to go. If you'd go with them, they might do it."

Boyce hurried off to Patrick's hut, Amber right on his heels. At Patrick's living quarters oil lamps burned, and they found Patrick, Ruth, and their family of orphans sitting in a circle on the floor, praying. "Come," Patrick said, taking hold of Boyce's elbow. "We've been waiting for you."

Amber inched inside behind Boyce, hanging

back, trying not to be in the way. Boyce went to Ruth, crouched in front of her, and caught her hands. "Jodene told me. She said you wanted me to go with you and Patrick."

Ruth's large brown eyes looked serious. "I love my cousin. I would love to share this time with her. And I want to marry Patrick without waiting until September. Yet I am afraid." A wry smile crossed her face. "It seems as if God is calling me home to face my demons, doesn't it?"

Amber realized the difficulty of Ruth's choice. Returning to the place where her life had been so cruelly changed would take great courage.

Patrick said, "I told her we will do whatever she wishes. I only want her to be happy. If you come, Boyce, we can go together as health care workers. Therefore, the visas into Rwanda will be easier to acquire. There is no danger in going there now, but it will take away your time from the irrigation project. We would be gone at least seven days. Four days for traveling, three at the village."

Boyce looked at his foreman. "The project is in good hands. I could spare a week." He turned back to Ruth. "The decision is yours. We'll both do whatever you want."

Tears made Ruth's eyes shimmer in the light. "In my heart, I want to go. It is foolish for me to be afraid of what happened years ago. I have not seen my family in a long time. There would be such a time of rejoicing for us to be together again . . . and for such a happy event as a double wedding." She slid her hand into Patrick's. "And once we are married, we can begin God's work in earnest. Yes," she whispered. "If you will come, Boyce, I will go."

"We'll go to Kampala and get our visas this week. The sooner the better."

An excited buzz circulated through the group, and laughter leaped from person to person as plans solidified. Amber stepped out of the shadows and cleared her throat. "Um—excuse me." All eyes turned toward her. She took a deep breath. "I—I'd like to come with you. Can I come to your wedding? Please?"

12

"Are you sure your mother approves of this trip, Amber?" Jodene stood at the foot of Amber's bed while Amber stuffed clothing into a duffel bag.

"I talked to her when we were in Kampala getting our visas. She was perfectly all right about my visiting Rwanda for a few days." Amber had played down the excursion to her mother, saying that it was a wedding party with a group going to a nearby African village. Was it Amber's fault that her mother automatically assumed Jodene was also going? "Ruth needs company on the trip," Amber told Jodene. "She shouldn't go alone with Patrick and Boyce. Besides, I'd love to take pictures of the wedding for Heather."

"Any word on your sister?"

"Not yet."

"I worried about Heather when she took off to Sudan to rescue Alice," Jodene said with a sigh. "Now I guess I'll have to worry about you, too."

"But things are different for me. There was shooting going on in Sudan."

"Don't ever assume Africa will remain peaceful. You never know when trouble will boil over—"

"No gloom and doom, please," Amber insisted with a radiant smile. "We're going to a wedding. Ruth's wearing a traditional Ugandan dress, but she's asking me for details about weddings in the States. Don't you see, Jodene? At last I have something to share with people. I mean, if Amber Barlow doesn't know fashion and trends, who does?"

Jodene laughed. "You are irrepressible. Very different from your sister."

"Is that a bad thing?"

Jodene considered Amber thoughtfully. "No. Heather was very dedicated, but also very idealistic. Maybe too idealistic for this kind of life. You're more practical, which will serve you better in the long run, I think."

Amber felt flattered. She hadn't wanted to be compared to Heather and found wanting.

"Well, life around here is different, all right, and personally, I don't know how you do it. My father always told me that I'd better marry a rich man because I have such expensive tastes."

"First you have to fall in love with a rich man, don't you?"

"A small detail." No matter how much she loved a guy, Amber realized she couldn't make the kind of sacrifice it took to live in a foreign country without the comforts and modern conveniences she'd enjoyed all her life.

"Well, there are few rich men in the mission field," Jodene added. "At least, they're not rich in the conventional sense."

"No problem," Amber said, wondering if Jodene's comment was her way of warning her not to fall for Boyce. "I'm sticking to my game plan. A long and happy life in close vicinity to a mall."

Jodene cocked her head. "We'll see," she said breezily. "Sometimes God has a way of changing our plans whether we're willing or not."

The next morning Boyce and Patrick packed the Jeep. Amber sat up front with Boyce while

Patrick and Ruth wedged into the back with baggage and sleeping bags, content to snuggle for the two-day ride to the Rwandan village of Ruth's uncle. They spent the first night in a small hotel in Kabale that had a long balcony stretching around the second floor, overlooking the street. Amber and Ruth settled into their room, then met Patrick and Boyce on the balcony, where they sipped colas and watched the sun set over the mountains.

The rich green rain forest hugged rising peaks covered with misty clouds, and the voices of rain frogs and crickets sang a song of welcome to the approaching night. As twilight deepened, the street filled with people, and small charcoal fires flared to life. Grilled food perfumed the air with savory scents.

Boyce dug out a map and flattened it on the table. "The village should be about here," he said, making a circle with his finger.

"Don't you know for sure?" Amber asked. The map was blank in that space.

"Old map," Patrick said. "As we get closer, people along the way will tell us. All we need do is ask for the house of Edward Kaumahome. He is the wealthiest man in the area, with the best farmland and the most cows. Three cows will be given as part of Ann's dowry. It will be a good start for her and her husband."

Heather had told Amber that Ugandans in the bush measured wealth by the number of cows they owned, but still it was odd to hear Patrick say it.

"You do not give cows away at weddings in America?" Ruth asked.

"If someone says the word *cow* at a wedding in our country, it's usually to describe an over-sized bridesmaid," Amber joked.

Boyce chuckled, but Patrick and Ruth gave her blank stares.

"You do not own a cow, Amber?" Ruth asked.

"No way. We have city ordinances against keeping livestock in our garages."

Ruth's incredulous expression turned to one of bewilderment. "But—But how can this be? You are a rich American. Where do you get your milk?"

It occurred to Amber suddenly that Ruth had asked her questions in complete innocence— she had absolutely no knowledge of dairy farms, grocery stores, refrigerated trains and trucks, or interstate highways. Amber cleared her throat and answered thoughtfully and gently, "Back home, milk comes in big plastic jugs. And the jugs are kept in special stores. I don't own a cow, Ruth, but I own a car that I drive to the store to buy the milk."

Ruth's eyes grew wide, and a lovely smile broke over her face. "Ahh! A car . . . you are a very rich American indeed."

With a lump in her throat, Amber said, "Yes, Ruth, I guess I am."

When Boyce and Patrick said good night, Amber and Ruth went to their room, a small cubicle with unpainted walls and two beds. The mattresses sagged pitifully, but the sheets were clean and smelled like sunshine. A wooden nightstand held a beat-up metal pitcher and bowl, which Ruth filled with water from the communal bathroom at the end of the hall. Amber remembered the bathroom at home that she shared with Heather—luxurious as a queen's by comparison. She washed her face, brushed her teeth with bottled water, and crept cautiously between the sheets.

Ruth clicked off the light, a bare bulb hanging from the center of the ceiling. Moonlight poured through the lone window, bathing the room in silver. The air felt warm, but not sticky or humid, and the scent of lemongrass drifted on every faint breeze.

"Are you excited about getting married?" Amber asked. They were to be in the Jeep by six in the morning, but she wasn't the least bit sleepy.

"I am anxious," Ruth said, her voice sounding hesitant in the dark. "I know there is much more to being a wife than the wedding ceremony."

"Boyce told me what happened to you when you were twelve. I—I'm very sorry."

"I have talked to many women who have been defiled by rape. I know all the things to say, to help victims with their pain." Ruth took a ragged breath. "But still, I wonder if I can be a proper wife to Patrick. He tells me he will be gentle with me. That he loves me. But still, sometimes in my bad dreams, I remember. In the dark places of my soul, I feel those men's hands. I remember how they held me down, tore my clothes. I remember how they hurt me." Her voice broke. "I cried for my mama. . . ."

Amber slipped out of bed and sat on the edge of Ruth's mattress. She took Ruth's hand clumsily, at a loss for words, not knowing how to help Ruth deal with her grief. Her experience extended only as far as listening to a girlfriend weep when some boyfriend had dumped her. Amber's response had consisted of trashing the guy and telling her friend she was truly cool and that the breakup had been the guy's loss.

Her only experience with real grief had come in fifth grade. A girl named Lisa had lost her mother in a car wreck. Amber recalled wanting to stay clear of her, as if Lisa's tragedy might somehow rub off on her if she got too close. As if Lisa's sadness might suck the class members under, like the vortex of water that gobbles a sinking ship. And so, with Amber's help, Lisa had been carefully ostracized, cut out of the circle of normal girls by the fear of contamination, until she had gone away. Now Amber was ashamed of the way she had acted. Ashamed and sad. She wanted so much to soothe Ruth, to protect the terrified child Ruth had been that night from the terrible thing that had happened to her. Yet it was as if she'd been struck dumb.

"It hurts my heart," Ruth whispered. "They took from me the treasure I wished to save for my husband. I know I must forgive them for what they did to me. There is no other way to leave the memories behind. And yet, tonight, I am sad inside. I am sorry for what was taken from me. What have I to give my husband now?"

Forgiveness? Amber could hardly comprehend it. Those men didn't deserve forgiveness. They deserved to die! "You have plenty to give him." Amber found her voice. "You have your heart to give him. You have your love, only for him. Those men stole your virginity, but not your love. That has always been yours to give away. Now you've given it to Patrick. And"— she paused, sensing that Ruth was listening— "you'll give him babies, too. A boy. A girl. Much better than many cows."

Ruth let out a tiny laugh. "We shall have cows, for we have no magic jugs filled with milk, only the udders of the cows to feed us."

"Just remember," Amber said, "Patrick loves you. Isn't that why you're going to your uncle's village? To pledge your love to each other forever?"

"Yes. Before my countrymen. Before God."

"You'll be a good wife, Ruth. You and Patrick will be happy. I know this because . . . well . . . just because I know these things."

The room fell silent. Amber watched the

moonlight move across the floor until it became a pale white sliver. Thoughts swirled in her head . . . thoughts of her parents, working side by side all their lives to build a place of safety and comfort for their daughters. Of Dylan, whom she'd liked but never truly loved. She was glad she'd always told him no when he'd pressured her for sex. And she thought of Boyce, too. Wondered if he thought her the silliest and most frivolous of girls. She had all but invited herself on this trip. Perhaps he thought her pushy. She'd hate having him think that.

"Thank you for listening to my heart's worries, Amber. It has helped to say them aloud," Ruth said, breaking the stillness. "I—I was afraid to say anything."

"Why?"

"You have no reason to listen to the thoughts of a girl such as I."

"I sure do! We're girlfriends," Amber insisted fiercely. "Girlfriends can say anything to each other. Repeat after me: 'Hey, girlfriend.'"

Ruth imitated Amber's intonation, then giggled. "*Rafiki*, that is 'friend' in Swahili."

"*Rafiki*," Amber repeated. "I'll remember it."

Darkness closed around the room as the moon slipped away from the window. Amber listened to the serenade of night creatures, felt her eyelids growing heavy.

"Goodnight, girlfriend," Ruth whispered.

"Goodnight, *rafiki*," Amber whispered back.

She returned to her bed and fell asleep to dream of a great white ship drifting on a bright blue sea, and of a man standing on the deck, shielded by shadows. She strained to see his face but couldn't. And no matter how hard she tried, no matter how close she came, his face would not come into focus.

13

Early the next morning, Amber and her friends drove off in a ground fog that rapidly dissipated as the sun rose over the African bush country. Midmorning, their Jeep was stopped at the Rwandan border for a check of their visas by an intimidating trio of border police wearing dark blue uniforms. Pistols hung from belts around their waists, and they balanced Uzi automatic weapons expertly in their hands.

Patrick spoke to them amiably in Swahili, offering permits and documents, making a great show of the Red Cross armbands the four of them had put on that morning. The police insisted on taking a look at Amber's passport, which Amber wore in a pouch around her neck, and Boyce's too. Finally the police returned all the documents, had a few more words with Patrick, and waved them through.

"Not a very friendly group," Amber said once they were well on their way.

"They are keeping out undesirables," Patrick said.

"And that's us?" She was insulted.

"It is their job to be suspicious."

"What did they say at the last?" Boyce asked, his face set like stone. "I caught some of it, but not all."

"They said to be careful. Bandits and marauders have been in the area. They reminded us that only a year ago, a group of French and British tourists were attacked and two were killed."

Amber felt a sick sensation. She turned, and the look on Ruth's face was one of fear. Amber's heart went out to her.

The roads in Rwanda weren't any better than the roads in Uganda and worsened when Boyce turned onto a dirt trail that zigzagged through the countryside. Amber had tucked her hair under a safari hat, wrapped a wet neckerchief around her throat, and slathered herself with sunscreen, but there was no protection from the dust. She took small, frequent sips from her water bottle; the inside of her mouth felt gritty.

She was surprised at the number of huts she saw as the Jeep bounced over the hard ground. The dwellings showed no sense of order, no sense of community, sitting alone on the plain as if dropped at random. Women tilled parched gardens, babies strapped to their waists. Children wearing frayed shorts and torn T-shirts herded clusters of goats under trees and fanned flies off grazing cattle. The few men Amber saw sat under trees, smoking and talking together. "Don't the men help out?" Amber asked.

"No, farming is women's work," Patrick explained.

"So what do the men do?"

"They marry," he said with a laugh. But Amber didn't think it was funny. She'd met too many women at the hospital clinic who were exhausted and worn out from hard work and childbearing before they were thirty.

Boyce stopped around noon, and the four of them ate a lunch of fruit and cold boiled rice. "There'll be a feast in the village after the wedding," Boyce assured Amber.

"Chicken?" she asked with a sinking sensation.

"Probably roasted goat," Patrick said. "Very delicious."

"Yum," Amber said while her stomach rebelled.

In the afternoon Boyce turned north and the scenery became greener, the land more hilly. About three o'clock Boyce pointed to a cluster of thatched-roof huts in the distance.

"My uncle's village!" Ruth cried. She stood, held on to the roll bar, and began to wave.

The Jeep halted in the center of the village amid a cloud of dust. People poured out of huts, smiling, chattering, surrounding the Jeep. Ruth leaped down and ran to a man and a woman who enveloped her with welcoming hugs. Amber found herself caught up in the joy of the moment, even though she couldn't understand a word that was being said. "They're glad to see us," Boyce told her with a broad smile.

Ruth introduced her parents and the members of her extended family. Amber's head swam with a deluge of names she would never remember.

"You are just in time for afternoon tea," Ruth's mother, Winnie, said in perfect English. "And we will discuss all the plans for the wedding."

She led them into the largest hut in the village, where a small table was set with a beautiful porcelain tea service. Amber found the contrast between the delicate cups, saucers, and teapot and the rough mud walls and packed earthen floor poignant—the old British custom seemingly archaic and quaint so far from its moorings of polite English society. Ruth and her cousin Ann held hands, and talk of the wedding bounced between two languages. Amber picked up only fragments of the conversation.

Finally she and Ruth were shown to their quarters, a hut divided into two areas by a colorful bolt of cloth hanging from a wooden beam that supported the thatched roof. Shoes were left by the front door. Woven straw mats and rugs covered the earth floor. On the other side of the curtain lay straw pallets. Amber dropped her backpack with a thud. "Our beds?" All at once she wished for the sagging, lumpy mattresses from the hotel.

"Yes," Ruth said. "The village is honored to have Americans for visitors, so a family has moved out in order for us to have their home during our visit."

"You grew up in a village like this?" Amber glanced around. One small window cut out of the hardened clayey mud allowed light and air into the room. The only other furniture consisted of a single chair and a small wooden table.

"Not one nearly so large and fine. Our home was much smaller, but I was happy there. Until the rebels came." Water had been placed in a basin, and Ruth indicated that Amber should wash her hands. As Amber knelt over the basin, Ruth said, "My uncle's village is successful because it has a steady supply of fresh water. In the bush, water is a most precious asset. That is why Boyce's work in irrigation is so important. Better access to water means not having to move away when the supply runs out."

Amber understood. Without water to nourish the people, crops, and animals, there would be no farming. "Uganda's greener," she said.

"Yes. In Uganda, water is more plentiful—" A giggle sounded behind them, interrupting Ruth. Amber turned to see a small girl balancing on crutches. "Rosemary?" Ruth said, her smile lighting up. "Is that you, cousin?"

The child hobbled forward, and Amber saw

that her back was severely twisted, her head permanently tilted to one side. Ruth knelt to hug her, then introduced her to Amber. "Pleased to meet you, Amber," the girl said with perfect diction and a radiant smile. "I have a new dress for the wedding. It is green with white flowers, and my mama bought it for me in Kigali at the big store. And I have shiny black shoes and new socks, too."

"I—I can't wait to see you all dressed up," Amber said, charmed by the child, shocked by her physical condition.

"I will come to your hut later and we will have a long visit," Ruth told the girl. "But now Amber and I must rest."

"Have a pleasant rest," Rosemary said, offering another heart-melting smile, and hobbled out on her crutches.

"How old is she? What happened to her?" Amber asked as soon as the child was out of earshot.

"She's seven, and she contracted TB when she was a baby. It affected her spine. Rosemary is one of the reasons I want to learn about medicine. Many problems can be prevented with the correct medicine given to the very young."

Amber knew that TB had been all but eliminated in the United States for years. Ruth's choice to devote herself to learning about medicine and helping not only relatives but strangers made perfect sense. Amber thought of her own sister. Suddenly Heather's feelings for baby Alice made perfect sense too. Saving one child in the midst of all these bleak problems seemed like a small thing, but surely it made a difference. And enough small differences could have a real impact. Amber felt proud of her sister. And her pride gave her courage. She looked back at Rosemary.

"She's adorable," Amber said, still shaken by the child's deformity. "There's absolutely nothing to be done to help her?"

"No. It is too late for Rosemary. She had no medicine when she needed it." Ruth sighed, then brightened. "I have chosen her to be the one who holds our wedding rings during the ceremony. She is excited."

Tears misted Amber's eyes. The difficulty of the trip; the simplicity of the village; the splendidness of the tea service; Ruth's kindness; the knowledge that she, Amber, as an honored guest, had been given the best the villagers had to offer; the sheer beauty of Rosemary's smile suddenly overwhelmed her and left her feeling humbled. "You've chosen well, Ruth, *rafiki*," Amber said. "She's the perfect ringbearer . . . the perfect choice. And I can't wait until tomorrow to attend the wedding of the year."

Both brides wore traditional Ugandan marriage dresses for the double cermony, which was held near the village in a small cinderblock church, where Ruth's father was the minister. People dressed in their best finery sandwiched themselves into the pews, stood along the inside walls, spilled out the doors, and clustered outside in the hot sun. To Amber it looked as if the entire countryside had turned out for the event. Amber and Boyce had seats in the same row as Ruth's family. When the pianist began playing "Jesu, Joy of Man's Desiring," on an old upright, all eyes turned to watch the bridal procession.

That morning, as Amber had watched a nervous Ruth dress, she'd said, "You're going to be fine. Just remember to keep smiling."

"Is this how brides in your country feel on their wedding day? All shaky on the inside?"

"Nerves are natural. Back home I get twitchy every time I have to dress up in a formal. I think it's a side effect of putting on panty hose. Anyway, I calm right down when my date hands me a present. Here. Wear this. It'll help *you* stay calm." Amber slipped a gold chain with a heart-shaped sapphire pendant from her neck and fastened it around Ruth's.

"It is beautiful!"

"Keep it. It's yours."

Ruth's eyes widened as she admired the necklace in a small hand mirror propped on the table. "I cannot take such a gift."

"But it's perfect on you. And it's the way we do things in America. On her wedding day the bride carries four things: something old, something new, something borrowed, and something blue. Now, your dress was your mother's, so it's borrowed, and your Bible is new. The necklace is old *and* blue, so there's both things in one."

"And this is your custom?"

"Absolutely."

Now, as Amber watched Ruth come down the aisle, she was certain she'd done the right thing. Never mind that she'd begged her parents last Christmas for the expensive necklace. It looked perfect on Ruth. She only wished Heather could be there to see the service.

After the ceremony, while the pianist played, the congregation sang songs and danced in the aisles. Finally the group broke up and returned to the village, where Ruth and Mary's families threw a giant party. On the outskirts of the village a great pit had been dug, and a glowing charcoal fire roasted several goats on a spit. Amber watched their charred carcasses being turned by several small boys, wishing she could sit down in a restaurant and order something off a menu.

"They *are* pretty tasty, you know," Boyce assured her. He offered her a warm soda from a nearby plastic bucket. "Barbecue's a Southern tradition. Even you folks in Miami must have cookouts in the summer."

"Hello—in Miami the meat is in cute little patty form, not on the hoof."

He laughed. "Well, they're going to slide a slab onto your plate, so tell them thanks. It would be a great insult if you didn't take any."

"Swell. What if I throw up? Will that be insulting too?"

"Bring it to me and I'll eat it for you."

"You must have an iron stomach."

"I'm from Alabama, where scorched meat is a way of life." He draped his arm casually over her shoulder. "By the way, I noticed you gave Ruth your necklace. That was nice of you."

"I couldn't let her only wedding present be some cows, could I?"

"Don't worry, they'll have plenty of gifts. When we get back, Jodene will throw a bodacious party for them. Paul's making them a wedding bed. He's carving the headboard himself."

"Ruth's nervous about that part. You know . . . the sleeping together. The sex."

"So is Patrick."

"Really?" Somehow the news relieved her. She didn't want Ruth to have a bad experience with the man she loved and wanted to be with until death parted them.

"Patrick loves her. He knows she'll have trouble getting over what happened. He won't hurry things. Plus, they have a lifetime to work it out. The right girl's worth waiting for," Boyce added.

Boyce's eyes were bright green, set off by a tan gained from hours of hard work under the African sun. She saw the outline of rock-hard muscle through his shirt, the golden hair of his forearms glinting in the light. His hands were work-worn and rough, his mouth dangerously close to hers. Her pulse pounded.

"How do you know when the right one comes along?"

"They say you just know."

"Do you believe that?"

A smile turned up the corner of his mouth. "With all my heart."

Amber woke with a start in the inky darkness of her room. After the banquet and party, each newly married couple had been loaned a special hut, where they were to celebrate their wedding night, and Amber had returned alone to the hut she'd shared with Ruth. She heard the noise of someone moving in her room, and suddenly, knowing she was no longer by herself, she was wide awake. Terrified, she opened her mouth to scream.

A large hand clamped down on her face. Boyce's voice whispered urgently, "Don't be afraid. It's just me. Get your things together quickly. We've got to get out of here."

14

"Do you understand what I'm telling you?" Boyce asked in the darkness.

Amber moved her head up and down, and Boyce slid his hand off her mouth. Her heart thudded crazily, and adrenaline flooded her body.

"I'm sorry to wake you up this way, but I couldn't risk you screaming."

"Wh-What's wrong?"

"A runner came—a friend of Ruth's family. He said some bad men, some very bad men," Boyce said with emphasis, "are headed this way. They heard about the wedding and figured there would be things for the taking. The villagers will try to protect themselves, but if they fail . . ." Boyce paused. "Well, let's just say it would be terrible if we Americans fell into their hands."

Amber trembled from sheer terror. "What are we going to do?"

"We're going to make a run for it. You and me and Patrick and Ruth."

"What do you want me to do?"

"Get your backpack, take only the essentials—one change of clothes, extra socks—and meet me outside the hut. And hurry."

He was gone. Amber scrambled to her feet, dressed in the dark, found her flashlight, and, keeping the light aimed at the floor, stuffed her backpack as he'd instructed. Her fingers felt cold and stiff, though perspiration poured off her face. She grabbed her passport and visa, insect repellant, sunscreen, a few T-shirts, socks, and her hat. She never thought once of what she was leaving behind. Outside, Boyce took her hand while the villagers scurried in the dark to take up defensive positions.

He led her to Ruth's parents' hut, where Ruth and Patrick waited. An oil lamp burned dimly, and one look at Ruth's face revealed that she was in worse shape than Amber. "We won't let anything happen to you," Amber said, putting her arms around her friend.

Boyce and Patrick crammed each backpack with bottles of boiled water and emergency rations. Amber recalled asking Jodene why they had to take so much extra stuff when they would be gone only a week, and Jodene had answered, "Always be prepared. What if the Jeep breaks down?"

"Is the Jeep ready?" Amber asked, longing to put distance between them and the village as quickly as possible.

Boyce never looked up. "I've disabled the Jeep. We'd be sitting ducks in it. We're going out on foot."

"But—But how will we know the way?"

He glanced up. "We have a compass."

Terror choked her. Winnie pulled Amber and Ruth into her arms. "God will protect you. He will watch over you."

"What of you all?" Amber asked.

"He will be with us, too."

A man entered the hut, carrying Rosemary. The little girl was crying. "The children have scattered into the bush to hide. She cannot go," he said, setting her down. "She will have to stay in the village."

Ruth knelt and smoothed Rosemary's tangled hair and looked around the room.

"We'll take her." Amber hadn't realized the words had come out of her. The others stared at her. With a decisive movement, she picked up the child. Rosemary seemed weightless.

"She will impede you," Winnie said. "We will try to protect her here."

"If she's captured, you know what will happen to her," Ruth said woodenly.

"It will happen to all of us," Winnie answered.

Amber interjected, "I won't let it." She gave Boyce and Patrick a pleading look. "Please. We must make a difference even for one child."

Boyce stood and hoisted two backpacks. "We'll take turns," he said. "I'll take your pack for now."

A man stuck his head in the doorway. "Hurry! They are coming through the bush. They have guns." The *pop, pop, pop* of gunfire sounded in the distance.

One more quick round of hugs; then Amber settled Rosemary on her hip and followed Boyce into the night. Shouting, running people almost collided with them. Several of the huts had been set on fire. "Diversion," Boyce shouted.

Crouching low, the five of them ran into the night, like leaves blown by a cruel wind.

Amber had no idea how long they darted through the bush, but soon her lungs felt on fire, her arms and legs screamed from exertion, and Rosemary felt like a lead weight. "I—I can't keep up . . . ," she gasped.

Boyce stopped, relieved her of the child, and helped her slip a backpack onto her shoulders. "We've got to keep moving," he said. "Stay low."

Ruth stooped over, panting hard, and Patrick adjusted her backpack. "I will carry it for you."

"No," Ruth said. "I can do it."

Amber heard the sound of more gunfire, and the sky behind them wore a halo of eerie red orange. Tears welled in her eyes. "Will they be all right?"

Boyce took long deep breaths. "Ruth's uncle has firepower too. He'll fight."

"Can we wait it out?" Amber asked. "Go back when the fight's over?"

"Can't take a chance," Boyce said. "We've got to keep going."

"Which way?" Amber asked. With only the light of the stars to see by, she had lost all sense of direction.

"North," Boyce said, hoisting Rosemary higher on his hip. He pointed toward a star, brighter than the others. "To Uganda."

* * *

Amber passed the point of exhaustion somewhere in the long night. She was disoriented and scared, and the backpack felt heavy as a boulder. Her shoulders and back begged for mercy, but she knew she didn't dare complain. This was a race for their lives. If the rebels caught up with them . . . *Pick up foot, put it down* became her mantra. The others were tired too, but to stop might be suicide. The village was far behind them by now, but in the dark they had the best chance of escaping detection.

She struggled over the rocky ground, stumbled, and fell with a cry. Boyce and the others huddled around her. She began to cry. "I—I'm bleeding." She was wearing a skort and strong hiking boots, but the sharp edge of a rock had sliced open her knee. "Maybe you had better go on without me. I'm just holding you up."

"No!" Boyce said. "No one gets left behind." He pointed toward the horizon on their left. The sky was turning gray and the stars were fading. "Dawn's coming. We'll need to find a spot to sleep."

With Ruth on one side of her and Patrick on the other, Amber hobbled after Boyce, who led the way to an outcropping of rocks shielded by another hill. They fell into an exhausted heap and struggled to catch their breath. As the light of day broke, Ruth leaned over to check Amber's knee. "The cut is not deep," she said. She unpacked a small first-aid kit, smeared the cut with ointment, and dressed it with a bandage. Amber felt nothing. She was beyond pain.

Beside her, Rosemary patted her cheek, making Amber feel like a baby. The child was comforting her instead of the other way around. Amber offered the little girl a brave smile. "It's much better now."

Boyce passed around a bottle of water. "Two swallows," he said.

Amber longed to gulp the entire bottle but passed it quickly to Ruth to keep temptation at bay.

"Do you think we got away?" Ruth asked.

"From the rebels, yes," Patrick answered. "Now we must get away from the sun."

"We'll only travel at night," Boyce said. "It'll be harder, but cooler. There could be other groups of bad guys out here. Remember what the border police told us."

"How far are we from the border?" Amber asked, her voice trembling.

"Maybe sixty, seventy miles. With God's help, we can do it."

Amber almost gagged. The distance on foot across rugged terrain seemed insurmountable. "Now what?" she asked faintly.

"First we sleep. Then we count up our rations and see how long we can go without hunting food and water. We don't have enough of either with us."

"I'm not hungry," Amber said.

"You will be," Ruth said, her gaze fastened on the unfriendly, scruffy landscape. "We'll *all* be very hungry before this is over."

Amber remembered stretching out and resting her head on the backpack, then nothing until Boyce shook her shoulder. "Time to eat," he said.

She climbed out of a stuporous sleep, disoriented and groggy. Every muscle in her body hurt. "Eat without me. I'll eat later." She turned over, seeking the warm embrace of oblivion.

"Come on, Amber. In another hour we're going to have to start moving again."

"I don't think I can."

"Please, Amber. Come with us." Rosemary's teary plea snapped Amber fully awake.

She groaned and sat upright. Ruth sat hugging her knees, and Patrick was sharpening a knife on a stone. "Look, I'm up," Amber told Rosemary.

Boyce passed around the water bottle, again restricting them to a couple of sips apiece. "Now," he said, "here's what we have to eat."

On the ground he spread out eight cans of potted meat, a crushed box of granola bars, ten packages of peanut butter crackers, and an assortment of dried fruit packets. They stared at the pitiful selection, which would have to sustain five people over however many days it would take to reach safety. "What? No goat?" Amber asked, which made the others laugh.

Boyce picked up a can of meat and pried open the lid with its tab key. He passed it to Rosemary, Ruth, and Patrick, who each picked out a chunk. It came to Amber, who fished out an unappetizing lump and handed it back to Boyce. He took what was left and bowed his head. "We need to thank the Lord."

For what? Amber wondered, then felt ashamed. They were alive and unhurt. That was something. They ate the meat; then Boyce took Patrick's knife and divided a granola bar into five slim servings. Amber chewed her portion slowly, savoring every sweet crumb. "Well, supper killed ten minutes," she said.

"How's your knee?"

She stretched it and winced. "Sore, but it'll be okay. Ruth fixed it."

Boyce looked toward the sun, which was beginning to set in the west. "We move in a half hour. I'll take Rosemary." He smoothed the child's matted hair. "You all right with that?"

"Very all right," the little girl said. She glanced back in the direction they'd come from. "I hope my mama and papa are well. I have prayed to Jesus to watch after them. And he will do it. I know he will. Jesus is with us, is he not, Mr. Boyce?"

Her question tugged at Amber's heart. She had no faith in heaven right now. They were on their own in a harsh and brutal place, like sailors cast overboard into a storm-tossed sea. A sea of dirt, rocks, heat, and danger. She tried to avert her eyes before Boyce read her feelings in them.

In the distance she heard a wild animal howl, and a new fear seized her. She had once read *The Call of the Wild* by Jack London, and now she recalled vividly the law of the wilderness: *Kill or be killed. Eat or be eaten.*

Boyce lifted Amber's chin so that she was forced to meet his gaze. "Yes, Rosemary. He is with us. God tells us, 'Fear not, I am with you. I will strengthen you. I will help you. I will uphold you with the right hand of my righteousness.' Don't ever forget that. We are *not* alone."

15

They moved forward under the cover of night, heading north, following Boyce's lead, stopping often to rest. Amber's thirst seemed unquenchable, but their stash of water bottles was so meager that she felt guilty even taking her allotted sips. She battled hunger, and images of food constantly flirted with her mind—fat waffles smothered in butter and syrup, crispy french fries with hamburgers, and slices of rich, red, juicy watermelon.

The night sounds of hunting animals frightened her, but when she mentioned it to Boyce he said, "They're more afraid of us than we are of them."

"Want to bet?" she countered.

They created a litter for Rosemary, similar to the ones villagers used to carry their sick to the hospital in Lwereo. Using sturdy tree limbs, strips of one of Boyce's cotton shirts, and grass that Ruth expertly wove into a mat, Boyce and Patrick carried the little girl by balancing the long poles on their shoulders. It was easier on her, and it helped them make better time.

Rosemary never once complained. Yet Amber knew the child hurt, because sometimes she heard her whimper. "Her bones are very fragile," Ruth explained during one of their rest breaks. "We must be careful not to break any of her bones."

By the time dawn approached on the fifth day, Amber was so weary that she had grown stuporous—absolutely numb. "I don't think I can go on," she confessed to Ruth once they'd settled beneath some concealing bushes and tall grass along the side of a hill to sleep.

"Yes, you can," Ruth said. "We are making good progress."

Amber didn't know how Ruth figured that. To her it seemed as if they were going around in circles. The scenery never seemed to change; the mountains in the distance never seemed to get closer. She recalled how Heather had gone off to some kind of boot camp before boarding the Mercy Ship. Amber had had no such preparation. Except for physical education class and a few paltry workouts in the gym at their house, she did little in the way of physical exercise. She vowed to herself that once she got home, she'd begin a training regime that would keep her in tip-top physical condition. *Home*. The thought of it made tears fill her eyes.

"Are you all right?" Ruth asked. The sun was rising, and the filmy grass had turned gold in the light.

Amber wiped her cheeks. "Sure. Just tired and hungry. This wasn't exactly how I planned to spend my time in Africa, you know."

"It is strange how things work out," Ruth said. She glanced toward Patrick, who, along with Rosemary, was sound asleep a few feet away. "I spent so much time thinking about my wedding night and how difficult it might be, I never thought that I might not have a wedding night at all."

"You never got to do *anything*?" Amber realized it was none of her business, but she couldn't stop herself from asking.

Ruth shook her head. "I dressed for bed, we lay in the dark talking for a long time. Then the runner came with the news about the rebels, so we had little time alone. And now we have no time at all." Ruth's smile looked sad and tired.

"Sometimes no matter how hard we try to plan our lives, the journey takes an unexpected road. The things we worry about never happen. The things that happen are the things we never think to worry about. It is a mystery."

Boyce squatted down beside them. "You both had better get some sleep before the sun gets too hot."

Ruth rubbed her eyes. "I will join my husband." She crawled to where he was lying and lay down next to him. She was sound asleep in seconds.

"I'm tired," Amber admitted. "But not sleepy."

"I know what you mean," Boyce said. "My eyes feel like sandpaper in a dust storm, but my mind won't shut off."

"I keep thinking about home. I'm supposed to graduate next month."

"You'll be back by then. Promise."

She shrugged wearily. "High school feels like part of another life. It's like I'm watching myself in a dream, except that it's not a dream. This is real and my other life is the dream." Her voice caught.

He put his arm around her. "You'll have a lot to tell your friends once you get back."

"We will get back, won't we, Boyce?"

"Never doubt it. I'll bet we're halfway there already."

She bent her head and started to cry. Hating herself for it, she crawled away to be alone but discovered that Boyce was right beside her. "Go get some sleep," she told him between sobs. "I'm just feeling sorry for myself. You don't need to waste time on me."

"You're not a waste of time, Amber. Not ever. And you can cry if you want to."

"Oh, as if crying's going to fix anything. And as if I don't look bad enough already. Now I'll have mud caked on my face." No matter how hard she tried, she couldn't shut off her tears. Her nose ran, and she wiped it unceremoniously on her sleeve.

"I think you're beautiful," he said.

"Oh, right!" She picked up a handful of dirt and tossed it on the ground, then scooted away from him. "How can you get near me? I haven't had a bath in days . . . my hair stinks . . . my clothes smell . . . I haven't brushed my teeth since the wedding . . . I—I hardly remember how I used to look." If she could just stop crying! She was going to wake up Ruth, Patrick, and Rosemary.

"I remember seeing you for the first time," Boyce said softly. "You wore pink. Pink shirt, pink shorts . . . even your toenails were pink. You looked like a cloud of cotton candy."

His reminiscence caught her off guard. "How did you remember that?" she asked in a quivery voice. "*I* don't even remember what I was wearing when we met."

"Because I thought you were the prettiest thing I'd ever laid eyes on."

Her insides turned to jelly, and more than anything, she wanted to curl up in his arms. "Well, close your eyes and envision that Amber, not this one. Okay?"

"But I like this one too."

"How could you?"

"Because this was the Amber who never thought twice about bringing a crippled child along when the easiest thing would have been to leave her behind."

Her tears had finally stopped, and she stared at him. "It was the only thing to do. You wanted to bring her too."

"Frankly, I never thought of it. But you did. And you thought of it instantaneously, without consideration for the risk, or the fear of her slowing us down. And without a single thought that we'd have to share our pitiful resources with her. And you know what that tells me?" She shook her head, too surprised to speak. "It tells me that you're beautiful, no matter what you look like on the outside. And it's made me a little bit ashamed of myself because I didn't think of it first."

"I—I didn't know what else to do."

His smile began slow, then broke across his face fully, lighting up his eyes. "I know. And that's what makes it good. It was spontaneous. And it was right."

Overwhelmed by his assessment, she drew away. He had a false picture of her and she knew it was time to set him straight. "Please don't go pinning any roses on me, Boyce." She took a deep breath. "Do you know why I really came to Africa?"

"Because Heather asked you to."

"That's what I told my parents and my friends. But mostly I came because I was bored. Isn't that the dumbest reason? Bored," she repeated. "At home I was bored with school, my friends, my boyfriend, my whole life. Now when I think about home, I can't re-member one single reason I had for being bored."

"It's hard to appreciate what we have at times. The first time I came to Africa, I thought I'd pop in, do some good deeds, then roll back home and pick up where I left off. But when I got home, I couldn't get this place off my mind. The friends I made, the work we did together . . . well, it all counted for something. Nobody at home understood. They wanted me to be the same good ol' boy, Boyce Callahan. But I wasn't. I lost him over here."

"Is that why you came back? To find him again?"

"No. He wasn't worth much." He grinned. "I like the new one better anyhow."

"Heather told me the same thing about herself. She felt changed inside once she'd come here. But it's been hard for me to understand it. I mean, she was perfect before she came. When she got back all she did was disappear into herself. And preach to us about what we should be doing with our lives."

"You sound like you were mad at Heather."

The sun had risen fully by now and heat was building, like a fire being stoked.

"Maybe I was," she confessed. "Just a little. I love her, you know. She's my sister. But Mom and Dad are always on her side. She's the star of the family and always has been. Sometimes I feel invisible."

"I wish I was more invisible in my family. I'm the oldest. I have three kid brothers and for me, it's like I have to do everything right. And perfectly. They get to make mistakes, but I don't. They get to pick what they want to do with their lives. I get to carry on my father's business. It's expected of me."

"I thought you *wanted* to be an engineer."

"I do, but I want to work over here, not in my old man's office. I want to make the lives of people like Patrick and Ruth better. I want to help kids like Rosemary live where they don't have to worry about starving to death because it hasn't rained and the crops have all died."

"Can't you tell that to your dad?"

"I have. But he doesn't hear me."

Just like no one truly listened to Heather, Amber realized. All Heather had wanted was for Alice to have surgery so that the baby could have an easier life. But for a long time, no one had paid any attention to Heather's pleas. And Amber felt like the worst offender, insisting that their sisterly relationship return to the way things had been before Heather had made her trip. She saw now that Heather couldn't have returned to that image of herself—her experiences in Africa had irrevocably changed her.

Amber said, "If Heather hadn't gotten sick, I would never have come over here. And I'd never have met any of you all."

"And you'd never have been trudging through the bush trying to escape from bandits," he added without humor.

"Well, I'm not bored."

He laughed.

"If I hadn't come, if I hadn't met you all, it would have been a big loss, you know. My loss." She had leaned her head against his shoulder, and her eyes grew heavy. Heat blanketed the air. Insects buzzed. Sleep began to overtake her.

"There must be something you regret about this adventure," he said, his lips grazing her forehead.

Her stomach growled. She stifled a yawn. "One thing. That day we went to the lake . . . I wish I had eaten that chicken."

16

They'd walked six nights straight when Boyce and Patrick decided they might be close enough to the Ugandan border to change their pattern. They would walk during the day from that point on. "I figure we've covered maybe eight to ten miles a night since we left your uncle's village," Boyce said, nodding at Ruth. "That means we've traveled close to the distance we had to come. At this point, we'd *like* the Rwandan border police to find us. They could escort us into Uganda."

"Where's the border crossing?" Amber asked.

"No idea. But police units regularly patrol the countryside, especially near Bwindi National Park."

"To hold off poachers," Patrick explained.

They all looked at the mountains as Boyce

continued. "But getting closer to the park means a longer walk. I think we should just keep heading in this direction." He pointed north.

"What about the bandits?" Amber asked.

"It's unlikely they'd take the chance of operating this close to the border. They prefer to stay inland, farther away from the authorities."

"By now," Patrick added, "we have been reported overdue. Perhaps the police will be searching for us on both sides of the border."

Amber hadn't thought about that, but of course it made sense. She'd lost track of time. They were to have been gone only a week. She counted up the days and nights and realized they'd been away from Lwereo twelve days—most of those days spent walking through the bush. And she also realized that by now Paul would have contacted her mother at the hospital in Kampala to say that the wedding party had not returned and that their whereabouts were unknown. She groaned. "My mother's going to *kill* me when we get back."

Ruth looked startled. "But why? You've done nothing wrong."

"It's a long story," Amber said with a sigh. "I have a history of goofing up. I had to take a vow

I'd be on my best behavior to come to Africa. I didn't expect things to get so messed up." Then another thought occurred to her. She grabbed Boyce's arm. "Heather! What if Mom knows something about my sister? I have no way of finding out how she's doing. This is awful."

"All the more reason to get out into the open," Boyce said. "Plus, we're almost out of supplies. We need to be rescued, and the sooner the better."

During their arduous journey, they had found berry bushes, root vegetables, and edible plants that Ruth had discovered growing wild. Just the night before, Patrick had hunted and killed a rabbit. That morning they'd built a fire and roasted it. Amber had not been the least bit squeamish about eating it either. In fact, although it had been chewy, it had tasted delicious.

"We're tired now," Boyce said, "so I think we should all get some sleep. Especially through the heat of the day. First thing tomorrow morning, we start hiking again."

He must have known they were running out of energy to take both a day and a night to rest, Amber thought. With rationed food and water, everyone's energy reserves were low. By now she was used to falling asleep at dawn and rising in the late afternoon. Total exhaustion made it easy. *Good training for all-night cramming at college, Daddy*, she imagined saying to her father.

Her feet throbbed from all the walking. She'd loosened the laces on her boots as far as she could and still keep them on her feet, but she promised herself that once she returned home, she'd soak her aching feet in warm water for days and pamper them with gobs of cream and colorful polish. They deserved it.

"At least the scenery's better," she said as she stretched out on the ground. The weather wasn't as hot and the landscape was greener, more lush looking.

"We'll note that in the travelers' guide," Boyce said with a yawn. Seconds later he was snoring.

In minutes they were all asleep. Except for Amber. Despite her weariness, she couldn't make herself go to sleep. Thinking about Heather had upset her, and new worries assailed her as well. If their mother knew Amber was missing, so did their dad. Her family had no way of knowing she was all right. Just as she had no way of knowing how Heather might have taken the news of her disappearance. Would it cause her sister anxiety and harm her further?

Stupid, stupid, stupid, Amber told herself. *I did a really stupid thing by coming to the wedding.* And yet, even as she thought that, she dismissed it. Would it have been any easier to wait at the Children's Home in Uganda, sick with worry about Ruth, Patrick, and Boyce? And what about Rosemary? Would she even have been with them if Amber hadn't come along? The questions swirled in her head like a dog chasing its tail. By the time the sun was high in the sky, she had no answers. She also had not gotten any sleep.

Sweat poured off her. She felt sticky and itchy all over. Finally, at her wits' end, she stood and looked around. The others were dead to the world, and she didn't want to wake them with her restlessness. In the distance she saw a large clump of green and decided to explore it. If she found anything of interest, they could all return in the cool of the evening. She headed straight for the verdant patch of woods.

The area was farther away than it had appeared, and it took her fifteen minutes to get to it, but once there, she was glad she'd come. The air was cooler, the ground covered with a downy, soft grass. She stooped, ran her hand across the velvet blades, and sighed with pleasure. This would be easier to sleep on than the ground where they were sleeping now. She looked up at trees that grew tall and leafy, their branches webbing overhead like a sheltering canopy. And she heard the distinct sound of running water.

Her pulse quickened. A creek? She followed the sound and soon came to a gurgling stream trickling over rocks in a small gorge. Water! She had found water. She couldn't wait to tell the others. She told herself to get moving, but the siren sound of moving water rooted her to the spot. She knew better than to drink the stuff, but if she could just put her feet in it . . . Quickly she sat and tugged off her shoes and soggy socks. She half slid down the embankment and stepped into the stream—and felt as if she'd slipped into heaven. The cool water flowed up to her ankles, caressing her throbbing skin. "Wait till you see what I've found," she said aloud.

She turned, and a movement on the other side of the ravine caught her eye. She froze, her heart thudding. The foliage shook and she heard twigs snap. An animal? Realizing she was completely out in the open, she stooped, attempting to make herself smaller. Her heart pounded crazily as a shape emerged. She caught a glimpse of a man dressed in camouflage clothing. It couldn't be the Rwandan police because they wore dark blue. This man looked like a soldier. He carried a rifle. And Ruth's tales of her long-ago encounter with Rwandan rebel troops washed over Amber like scenes from a bad horror movie.

Bile rose in her throat. Maybe he wouldn't see her. Maybe he'd pass right by and never look down. She scrunched lower without taking her eyes off him. But he did look down. For an instant their gazes locked. His rifle came up. And in that split second Amber knew what she had to do. She ran.

"Simama! Simama!" he shouted.

She didn't know what he'd said. She didn't care. She only knew she had to lead him away from her sleeping friends. She scrambled up the embankment, oblivious of the sharp stones and dead branches that scraped and cut her hands and feet.

She heard the crack of the rifle, and a bullet

whizzed past her head. She dove over the top of the gully and dropped, crawling on all fours to the trunk of a tree, panting for breath. She heard him crashing behind her through the undergrowth. A second bullet fired, scraping bark off the trunk.

Terror tore at her insides. *I'm going to die!* He was going to kill her, shoot her to death when she could very well be a day's walk from safety. But if he killed her, it would be better than if he captured her. She was sure of that much. She wanted to get away but didn't know how. She wanted to hide but didn't know where. She wanted Boyce.

Another soldier materialized, then another. The woods were swarming with them. She'd foolishly fallen into a nest of hostile soldiers.

She saw two armed men coming straight toward her and struggled to cover herself under a heap of dead leaves. She lay flat, her face buried in a pile of moldy, rotting leaves, eyes shut tight, gasping like a cornered animal. She had nowhere to turn, no one to rescue her. They would kill her. Or worse.

A harsh male voice boomed down at her in a language she did not understand. Yet she knew the tone. It told her, *Get up. I've got you.* She heard the sound of a gun being cocked.

Amber sucked in her breath, opened her eyes, and saw the dark curved tops of military boots directly in front of her nose. *If you're real, God, help me.* The toe of the boot moved the rotting leaves around her face.

Time seemed to slow. " *'Fear not. I am with you. I will help you.'* " She heard Boyce's voice as clearly as if he'd been next to her. Defying all reason, a steely calm came over her. She gritted her teeth with determination. No matter what happened to her, she'd make them believe she was alone. And she wasn't going to die like some trapped, cowering animal, either. She raised one hand, reached inside her shirt with the other, and very slowly pulled out her American passport, still hanging on a dirty string tied around her neck. With both hands above her head, she held the booklet emblazoned with the American eagle aloft and staggered upright. She raised her eyes and stared up the long black barrel of the rifle.

"*Rafiki.*" Amber used the only word of Swahili that came to her mind. "Me, *rafiki.*"

17

"You are American?" the soldier asked in English.

"Yes," Amber said. The sound of her own heart pounded in her ears.

"But what are you doing in the bush?"

"I'm lost. I'm trying to get back to Uganda."

The soldier lowered his rifle. "But you are *in* Uganda."

"I am?" They had crossed the border and not known it. Tears welled in Amber's eyes.

"Are you the lost lady from Lwereo?"

She nodded, overcome with emotion.

"Where are your friends?"

She hesitated.

"We have been looking for you for many days, lady. You all must be very tired."

"Very tired," she echoed.

A grin split his face. "Welcome to Uganda."

* * *

Amber and her friends rode all the way into Kampala in a military convoy made up of Jeeps and two trucks full of Ugandan soldiers. The men made a great fuss over them, gave them food and water, and lavished candy on Rosemary, who'd tucked herself shyly under Ruth's arm. Against all odds, Amber fell asleep in the back of the truck, her head resting in Boyce's lap.

Once they arrived in the city, they were taken to the hospital, where a medical team checked them over and pronounced them dehydrated but in good condition considering their ordeal. Amber's cuts and scrapes were thoroughly cleaned and slathered with antibiotic ointment. She was also given a tetanus shot. When she got on the scale, she was shocked to see that she'd lost twelve pounds. "However, I don't recommend it as a weight-loss program," she told the nurse, who nodded in agreement. Amber also learned that her mother had returned to the Children's Home to await word from the soldiers who'd been sent out to search.

At the American Embassy, the five of them were greeted by photographers and newspeople. Amber felt overjoyed to be safe again, alarmed when she heard that their nighttime escape from invading marauders had captured world attention. That meant that everyone in Miami knew what had happened. There really would be no glossing it over to her parents.

"Almost a week in the bush—how did you do it?" one reporter asked.

Boyce told them that God had watched over them, protected them, and given them strength every day. But he also told them he'd once been a Boy Scout and had remembered his training. Patrick and Ruth had both been raised in the bush, so they too had survival skills. Only Amber felt as if she'd contributed nothing to the group's overall welfare.

When the session broke up, Ruth asked a reporter, "Can you tell us what happened to the village?"

"It defended itself bravely," he answered. "They had a stash of firearms the rebels weren't expecting. Rwandan military showed up the next day. Turned out they'd been trailing the rebels for weeks. These guys had already killed some tourists on safari, burned and looted a couple of smaller villages."

"How many deaths?"

"There were fifteen casualties, most of them on the rebel side."

"Do you have a list of the dead villagers?"

He handed her an Ugandan paper and she skimmed the article with a worried gaze while Patrick held her hand. Amber held her breath. Finally Ruth looked up with a trembling smile. "None of my family are on the list."

An embassy spokesperson arranged for a van to take them to Lwereo the following morning. "But first, a hot bath and clean clothes," he said. "We've made arrangements for you to stay the night at the Hilton."

By the time they reached the hotel it was almost nine in the evening, and Amber was dizzy with fatigue. "I don't know how I'll sleep tonight without you guys around," she told Boyce in the hall, while Ruth and Rosemary took the first showers. The girls had been given a sumptuous suite, Boyce and Patrick another down the hall.

"And I don't know how I'll fall asleep in a soft bed instead of on the hard ground."

"Well," she said thoughtfully, "I did want to talk to you about something."

"What now? You've got that look on your face."

"What look?"

"The one that tells me you're cooking up some wild plan."

"Not too wild. I'm too tired to think too wild. But I do I have an idea."

"Go on."

"First I'm going to take the longest hot bath on record. Then I'd like to bring myself and Rosemary to your room and put Patrick in our room with Ruth. They—um—never had that honeymoon night, you know."

An impish grin lit Boyce's face. "You'll give up your cushy bed for Patrick and Ruth?"

"No . . . you'll give up yours for me and Rosemary. Don't worry, we'll pitch you a pillow on the floor."

Boyce laughed. "I never guessed you were such a romantic."

"They deserve it, don't you think?"

"What I think is that you're pretty special." He drew her closer.

"Careful . . . I smell like the bottom of a compost heap."

Boyce shook his head and raised her chin with his forefinger. "I don't care."

Her breath caught as she realized he intended to kiss her. Her knees went weak, and her pulse quickened. "Um—can this wait until I'm more presentable?"

"No way." His mouth hovered above hers. "But I'll make you a promise: Once you *are* presentable, count on it happening again."

The following morning Amber, Rosemary, and Boyce went to the hotel restaurant for breakfast. "I told Patrick and Ruth to meet us here. But I told them not to hurry," Boyce said. His suggestive grin made Amber blush.

"No hurry for me," Amber said. "I only have to face my mother today. Come on, Rosemary, let's go check out the buffet."

The child had been given a new pair of crutches at the hospital, and she hobbled to the long table set with a banquet of food. Her eyes grew round. "Who is coming to eat with us?"

"Just the people in the hotel. What would you like?" Amber picked up a plate.

"Not the whole city of Kampala? There's enough for everyone, I think."

The realization that Rosemary had never seen so much abundance in her brief lifetime moved Amber. "Well, right now, there's only us, so let's try a few of my favorite things and see how you like them." She took another plate and proceeded to pile both with every kind of fruit on the table. Next she loaded up on scrambled eggs, rice, pancakes in warm syrup, bacon, ham, cheese and hash browns.

When she set the plates on the table, Boyce looked startled. "Did you leave any for me?"

"It's every man for himself," Amber said. She cut up the meat for Rosemary. "Try this." With much satisfaction, she watched Rosemary eat heartily.

"My turn," Boyce said, scooting out of the booth.

When Boyce returned, Amber asked him, "Do you realize this is the very same place Heather rested with baby Alice when she brought her out of Sudan?"

"I guess it is. Small world."

"It gives me a spooky feeling. Like we're both tied to this place somehow."

"It's possible."

Amber shook her head. "I hope not. Once I get home, I'm never leaving again."

"Heather couldn't wait to get back."

"I told you, my sister and I are different people. We want different things."

"You're not eating much." Boyce changed the subject.

She shoved her plate aside. "I dreamed of food when we were out in the bush. Now I'm not really hungry. I guess my stomach's shrunk."

"You're nervous about facing your mother, aren't you?"

Of course he'd figured it out. Amber said, "She's going to chew me out for taking off in the first place."

"She knew you were going. No one could have predicted the raid on the village."

"Yes, but I *may* have led her to think there were more people going than just the four of us."

"Well, if it will help, I'll tell her you were the hero that got us rescued. I'll tell her your bravery to go exploring by yourself made the difference."

She heard recrimination in his tone and knew it was justified. She'd put herself in life-threatening danger by wandering off on her own. "What you're saying is that if I'd stayed put, we'd still have been found, and I might not have gotten shot at and scared half out of my head."

"It gives me chills to think that you came so closed to being killed," he confessed. "But we can't go back and redo things, Amber. It worked out. Thank God you're alive."

She drummed her fingers on the table, then decided to tell him everything. "I prayed, you know. When I thought I was going to die, I asked God to help me. Inside my head, I heard you telling me not to be afraid, and suddenly I wasn't."

He put down his fork. "God's going to make a believer out of you yet."

"I think he already has. I just can't figure out why he's bothering with me."

"Maybe God's saved you to do something special for him."

His interpretation startled her, but before she could discuss it, Patrick and Ruth walked into the dining room. Amber jumped up and ran to them. "You two look wonderful!" she cried, hugging them both.

"We feel wonderful," Patrick said with a laugh.

Amber glanced anxiously at Ruth, wondering if she'd done the right thing by suggesting that they spend the night alone together. What if Ruth had not been ready? "Get the buffet.

Rosemary and Boyce are already chowing down."

Patrick kissed Ruth's cheek, then went to join Boyce, who'd returned to the buffet line when Amber had abruptly left the table. Amber hung back. She took Ruth's hand. "I—I have to see for myself that you're all right."

Ruth offered a beautiful smile. "I am a wife now in every way. There were no bad memories to hurt me, only the love of my husband to heal me."

Tears brimmed in Amber's eyes. "I'm happy for you both."

Ruth hooked her arm through Amber's. "Now, let us eat. Does this buffet have any roasted goat? I hardly got to taste it on my wedding day, you know."

It was afternoon when the van pulled into the town of Lwereo. Amber licked her lips nervously. Soon she'd be facing her mother's wrath. Soon she'd know all about Heather. She couldn't have one without the other.

Boyce put his hand on Amber's shoulder. "Remember, I'm here beside you."

"Thanks," she said gratefully.

But when the van pulled through the gates

of the compound, Amber couldn't believe her eyes. Throngs of cheering, waving people lined both sides of the dirt road, waving yellow ribbons. Every child, every family unit member, every worker on the irrigation project, even workers from the hospital had turned out to welcome them. Patrick and Ruth leaned out the windows and clasped hands with their friends. Boyce gave a high five to everyone he could touch. Rosemary stared at the crowd in awe.

The van slowed to a crawl and stopped in front of Paul and Jodene, standing out in their front yard. Their three sons pulled open the doors and, like overeager puppies, hurled themselves across the passengers' laps.

"We saw you on the news," Samuel, the youngest, yelled.

"Amber's mother bought us a TV!" Dennis shouted.

"And Dad turned on the generator so we could watch," Kevin finished.

Amber only half heard them. She was looking out at her mother, who stood off to the side, tears streaming down her cheeks. Suddenly Amber was crying too, apprehension over their reunion vanished. She jumped out of the van and ran into her mother's open arms.

"Oh, dear God, I thought I'd lost you," her mother sobbed.

Amber was crying so hard, she was shaking. "Mom . . . I—I'm sorry—"

"You're safe. That's all I care about. I was so worried, so scared." Her mother kissed her and hugged her until it hurt. "I don't know what I'd've done if . . ." She didn't finish the sentence.

"It's over, Mom. We made it out and it's over."

Her mother held her at arm's length. "No, it isn't. We've got to catch the first plane out of here."

Amber's heart constricted. Her mother's eyes changed from relief at seeing Amber to worried pools of grief. "What's wrong?" Amber asked urgently.

"Heather's critical."

18

"You want some magazines for the trip?" Amber's mother asked. They stood in front of a newsstand inside London's Gatwick Airport, looking at its display of international newspapers. YOUTHS SURVIVE ORDEAL IN AFRICAN BUSH, *USA Today* declared in bold lettering. "Apparently you've made the news in seven languages."

"Do I care?" Amber said. She could hardly believe that the headline referred in part to her. All she cared about at the moment was getting home. She and her mother had packed and left Uganda in two days, boarding the already sold-out airplane to London via special arrangement by the American Embassy.

Amber had talked to her father on the satellite cell phone the night they returned to

Lwereo. "How's Heather?" had been Amber's first words.

"Not good. How are *you*?" She heard so much emotion in his voice that she almost dissolved into a puddle of tears.

"I'm all right, Daddy . . . just a few cuts and bruises. Can I talk to Heather?"

"She's in ICU, and in isolation. She's very weak."

"Tell her I'm coming. Tell her to hold on till I get there."

"She's trying, baby. She's really trying."

"A good book might keep your mind busy." Her mother tried again to interest Amber in something from the newsstand.

"No, Mom. I'm going to try to sleep on the plane." The long flight stretched ahead like an eternity.

Her mother sighed wearily. "Me too. I sure didn't get much sleep when I was in Africa, and I'm sure we won't be getting much in Miami."

"It feels weird to be back in civilization," Amber said. In the crowded London terminal, she felt claustrophobic. The pressing crush of bodies was a far cry from the lonely, sweeping landscape of Africa. Cell phones rang, announcements crackled in several languages over the PA system, luggage on clattering wheels was pulled past them. Amber almost clamped her hands over her ears to shut out the racket.

"I felt the same way when I returned from my stint in the Peace Corps. A person gets used to all that quiet. Noise . . . it's one of the trade-offs for our modern lifestyle." Her mother paid for several newsmagazines. "Come on, they're boarding our flight."

They went to the gate and stood in line. Amber already missed her friends, unable to forget their tearful goodbyes at the Children's Home.

"Please let us know about Heather," Jodene had pleaded. "Tell her we're all praying for her. She can lick this thing. I know she can."

Patrick and Ruth had wept openly and without shame. "I will not forget you," Ruth said. "You have done so much for us, as well as for Rosemary. So much has happened. I wish that you could stay, but I know you need to go to your own family. *Rafiki*—girlfriend."

"I hope you and Patrick get your own church and start a healthy, beautiful family.

Ruth smiled through her tears. "And you and Heather will always be part of our family."

"Maybe someday the two of you can come visit America."

"I would like that."

Patrick had added, "I've gone to college in Boston, but I have never seen the South. Perhaps one day we will come calling."

"You'd better, because I won't be coming back to Africa, and I don't like thinking we won't see each other again."

"In the next life, we will," Ruth had said, giving Amber's hands a squeeze. "May God be with you, Amber."

Once aboard the plane, Amber shut her eyes and revisited her memory of saying goodbye to Boyce. The night before, he had walked with her into the field where he'd taken her on her first night. The change in the field had been dramatic—the irrigation canals were dug, the earth tilled and turned, the reservoir built and waiting for the rainy season. Moonlight spread across the waiting ground like golden cream. Boyce had said, "My work here is finished. By December this field will be planted and thick with crops. It gives me a good feeling."

"What will you do now?"

"Go back to school, I reckon. I still have several semesters before I graduate. After that, on to Dad's firm in Birmingham."

"Well, I'm sure this project will earn you the credits you wanted. What about our little side trip?"

"I expect it to earn me *extra* credit. How about you? What are you going to do?"

"After Africa, graduating and finding a college seems tame. I don't know what's going to happen if Heather—" She'd stopped herself, unable to say the words.

"No matter what happens to Heather, you have your life to lead, Amber. You'll go on."

"I don't know how. My first memories are of Heather. Of her holding my hand and playing with me." She started to cry, and Boyce held her against his chest. She heard his heart through the fabric of his shirt, felt her tears soak into the material.

"You tell that sister of yours to get well."

"If only she'll listen to me. She never has before."

"Take care of yourself," he said.

"No problem. I excel at some things."

He kissed her forehead.

"Not good enough," she'd told him. She'd put her hands on either side of his face and stood on tiptoe. "This is for taking care of us out there in the bush. We'd never have made it without you." She'd kissed him thoroughly, stepped away, and said, "I love you." Then, without letting him see her cry, she had turned and run back to the guest house. And out of his life.

The jet from London touched down at Miami International Airport just shy of three in the afternoon. It took another hour to get through customs, but once they were through the line, Ted Barlow was waiting for them at the baggage claim carousel. To Amber it looked as if her father had aged ten years since she'd last seen him. He was thinner and looked haggard.

He kissed them both. "Thank God you're home." He turned to Amber and ran his hands along her arms as if examining her for himself.

"I'm fine, Daddy. All my parts are still in working order."

"You're getting a complete physical as soon as I can arrange it."

"Whatever. Can we just go to the hospital?"

Janet fired questions during the drive through heavy traffic to the hospital. Amber tried to keep up, but her brain felt sluggish. She felt as if she'd been away years instead of just weeks, more like a visitor than a person returning home. The world she'd grown up in looked surreal—too hot, too bright, too noisy.

The colors were garish and cheap, the roads too wide, too crammed, an ocean of concrete instead of rich red earth studded with green.

At the hospital Ted took them up to the ICU, pausing at the forbidding door. "You're going to see Heather through a glass window. When she's awake she's coherent, and she can see you and talk to you through the speaker on the wall. Just push the button when you want to be heard."

"What does she know?" Janet asked.

"She knows it's bad."

Amber felt cold all over. "I want to hug her."

"Later. You have to go through sterility procedures. Her immune system is wiped out. Any germ can destroy her, even one from a common cold."

Amber walked to the window between her parents, holding their hands. Her knees went weak when she peered inside. Heather lay on a hospital bed, surrounded by equipment. She remained but a shadow of herself, wasted except for her abdomen—it was distended. Her hair had been cropped short, her skin was tinged yellow, several IVs ran into her arms, and clear tubing attached to a urine bag hung from below the sheets.

"Oh, my baby," Janet whispered. "Oh, my poor, poor baby."

Amber felt sick to her stomach. How could this be her sister? Heather resembled a limp, grotesque marionette. "Is she awake?"

"Push the button and talk to her." Ted motioned to the speaker box.

Amber pressed the button. "Hey, sis . . . guess who's here?"

Heather's eyelids fluttered open and she smiled. Only then did Amber see a flicker of her sister's former beauty. "Amber . . . Mom . . . can you come inside?"

"Dad says later." Amber's legs quivered from the strain of holding herself rigid. If she didn't, she feared she'd fall apart.

"Wasn't Africa wonderful? Did you have fun?"

Amber glanced at her father and he whispered, "I didn't tell her about your being lost."

"Wonderful," Amber said into the speaker. "Everybody there is praying for you."

"That's good. Can't have too many prayers." Heather's eyes closed, and Amber realized she was gathering her strength.

"I saw baby Alice right before we left. She's looking fine. Mom really did an awesome job of fixing her palate."

"I knew she would."

Janet stepped up to the box and relieved Amber's cramped finger. "Hi, honey. Mom here. You were right about getting back to my roots. I worked nonstop, but I fixed a lot of kids, corrected plenty of birth defects. And you know what? It felt good."

"I wish—" Heather stopped, then started again. "It would have been nice to go as a family."

"We can still do that."

"I don't know, Mom. I'm so tired."

"Well, I didn't mean right now."

Heather's eyes closed again, and Amber stepped away from the window. She couldn't bear to watch any longer. She didn't need a medical degree to know how sick Heather was. Or how useless it was to expect her to recover. Heather was dying. And all the medicine in the world, all the doctors and their expertise could not save her.

Amber went home with her parents for the night because they made her. She'd wanted to camp out at the hospital, but her father wouldn't hear of it. "Get some rest. Come back tomorrow," he said. "If you want to see any of your friends—"

"No." She interrupted him. "I don't want to see anyone. I'd just as soon not have them know I'm home."

"All right." He raked his hand through his hair and rotated his shoulders wearily. "Why don't we all get some sleep?" His suggestion made sense. Amber's internal clock was seven hours ahead of his, which made it one in the morning, Ugandan time. "Sleep in tomorrow, if you can. Drive to the hospital when you're rested. Your car's gassed and ready to go."

Amber agreed and went to her room, cool, quiet, spacious, awash in shades of lime and blue. After the bedroom of the guest house, it seemed obscenely huge. How much space did she really need? In Africa whole families lived in huts smaller than her room. "Quit it," she said to her reflection in the mirror. "You sound like Heather after she first came home." Her heart contracted as she remembered how sick her sister had looked that afternoon.

She wanted to talk to Boyce and actually picked up the telephone before she remembered he was three thousand miles away. *Bad idea anyway.* They'd already said their good-byes and gone their separate ways.

Without bothering to undress, Amber lay down on her bed. She felt as if the hard ground in Africa had been friendlier. There it had been only her body that was miserable. Here it was her very soul.

19

"I'm not afraid of dying, sis. I just regret not being able to do all the things I wanted to do with my life."

Heather's words did nothing to comfort Amber. She had stood at the window the next morning watching her sister sleep for a long time, and when Heather finally woke, Amber had complied with the necessary procedures and come into her isolation room. "Is this what I came home to hear you tell me?" Amber asked now. "I don't want you to die. Did you ever think about that?"

"We don't always get what we want."

"You're not giving up, are you? Because if you are—"

"What'll you do? Kill me?"

The absurdity of her anger made Amber pause. Heather was right. It wasn't as if Heather had any control over what was happening to her body. "Sorry," Amber said, hanging her head. "Let's start over, all right?"

"Okay . . . for starters, do you have any idea how silly you look in that getup?"

Amber wore a too-large paper gown. Latex gloves, a paper hat, and a special mask completed her ensemble. She twirled and struck a fashion pose. "I begged for something trendy, but this is all they had."

"That's better. Now, tell me all about Africa. Especially about you and Boyce."

"I'm crazy about him." Amber confessed her heart. "But what's the point? He has his whole life planned out. I still don't know where mine's going."

"Didn't anything in Africa get to you?"

"Of course it did. I haven't got a heart of stone." Amber told Heather about Ruth, Patrick, and Rosemary. She told her about their midnight run for their lives, about walking through the bush for six nights, looking for help and a way back into Uganda. Now that she was safe, she didn't see that Heather's knowing could cause any harm.

"And you thought you were going to be bored."

"No, boredom wasn't much of a problem. Except I can't say much good about the food."

"You nut!" Heather's eyes fairly glowed. "I wish I could have been with you."

"Don't think I didn't wish you were too. I figured I was going to be hanging around a hospital doing good deeds. Instead I was hanging around the bush eating strange life-forms."

Heather laughed, a sound that made Amber feel wonderful. "I kept asking Dad why you and Mom weren't home when you were supposed to be. Everyone thinks that just because I'm sick, I lose track of time. But I knew something was going on no one was telling me about. I thought Mom had gotten bogged down in an extended surgery schedule. I had no clue *you* were the one with the problem. So you had to make a run for it through the bush. And you did it. I'm impressed, sis."

Amber grinned, proud that she had pleased her sister. "The others get all the credit—especially Boyce. I just tagged along."

"Back to Boyce. Does he know how you feel about him?"

"Sure does—I made a fool of myself. I told him I loved him."

"Do you?"

Amber nodded. "I remembered what you told me about wishing you'd said it to Ian. I didn't want him to return to his real life without knowing how I felt. So I said it. And ran for cover."

"What if he feels the same way?"

"I'd be shocked. He's out of my league."

"I felt the same way about Ian. At least you laid your cards on the table."

Amber patted Heather's hand. She could tell that her sister's burst of energy was waning. "I'll come back later this afternoon."

"I'd rather you stayed. Until I go to sleep." Heather reached over to the morphine infusion pump and pressed a button. "My happy juice," she explained. "I hurt a lot inside. This stuff really helps."

Amber couldn't hold back the film of tears that glazed her eyes. Quickly she wiped them away. "I'll sit right here," she said, leaning back in a chair.

"Tell me more about Africa," Heather asked. "Tell me about the land, the people you met . . . Ruth's village. Tell me about . . . the Children's Home. Tell . . . me . . . please . . ." Her eyes drooped and closed.

Amber stroked Heather's thin hand and began to describe everything she could recall, no matter how insignificant. She continued to talk long after Heather was asleep. Long after her voice faded from the weight of emotion, while her heart trembled with memories.

Amber's high-school friends found out she was home and began to stop by the house in a steady stream. "I cut articles out of the newspaper about you being lost over there," Kelly burbled when she found Amber out by the pool. "I was so, like, totally scared. I mean, you could have died over there! So tell me, what was it like? I've got all afternoon."

"It wasn't so bad. The papers played it up. We ran from some rebel soldiers. We walked back to Uganda. End of story." Amber was reluctant to talk about Africa with any of her friends. She wasn't sure why. Her experiences ran deep, close to her heart. Her friends wanted a sensational story, and she wouldn't give it to them.

"That's all you've got to say?"

"I've got other things on my mind, okay?"

"You mean Heather. We're all really sorry about your sister, you know. Liz and Brooke and I tried to visit her in the hospital, but they wouldn't let us in the ICU because we weren't family."

"That was nice of you. I'll tell her you tried."

"Um—are you coming back to school?"

There were two more weeks of classes, but Amber wasn't about to return. "Don't need to. I passed all my finals before I left, remember?"

"Well, sure, but you could have lunch with us. Oh, and there's a party at Brooke's step-dad's lake place Saturday night. Why don't you come? Dylan's going to be there, and he's asking about you."

"Is that supposed to make me jump for joy? I could care less about Dylan."

"He and Jeannie broke up right after the prom."

Amber sighed. "Kelly, we've been friends for a zillion years, so I feel like I can be honest with you. Truth is, I don't want to party. I don't care what Dylan does with himself or who he dates. I don't want everybody hanging around asking me a bunch of questions. My sister's really sick, and she's the one I want to be with now. So please back off. And tell the others to give me lots of space."

Kelly looked shocked, then miffed. "Well— um—all right. I'll spread the word: Leave

Amber alone." She stood up. "See you at graduation."

"Whatever." Without regrets Amber watched Kelly leave, and as the door shut behind her, Amber felt as if the door to her once-perfect high-school life had also closed. She stood in a no-man's-land, unable to reconnect with her former world, unsure of how to live in her current one.

Amber went to the hospital with her parents every night, and after each visit she would say, "Heather looked stronger, don't you think?"

"About the same," her father would reply.

When he'd said it one too many times for Amber's liking, she erupted. They'd just walked into the kitchen together. Enraged, she flung her purse onto the kitchen counter. "You always say the same thing. I think she's looking better. Don't you, Mom?"

"I think having us with her again has helped her rally. It's lifted her spirits."

"See, Dad, Mom thinks so too."

He shook his head wearily. "Have it your way." He picked up a bag from the desk. "I keep forgetting to give these to you. It's your graduation announcements. The ceremony's been scheduled for next Sunday in the county auditorium. You've gotten some messages on the answering machine from your friends about all-night parties. If you want—"

"Would you and Mom be too disappointed if I didn't walk?"

Her parents exchanged glances. "Amber, high-school graduation is a major milestone," her mother said. "You've made it through twelve years of school, and we're proud of you. Not walking the aisle and getting your diploma won't influence what's happening to Heather."

"Is that what you think I'm doing? Sacrificing for Heather? Well, I'm not. I just don't want to go. The school can mail my diploma to me."

"Yes, but—"

Amber stamped her foot. Her nerves were on fire, stretched and ready to snap. "Didn't you listen? I don't want to go. It's not important to me. Please, don't make me!"

Her father moved swiftly to put his arms around her. She fought him but finally began to cry. "Shhh, baby," he said. "It's okay. Really. We're not going to make you do anything. Calm down. If you don't want to attend the ceremony, you don't have to."

She clung to him, sobbing, all her energy gone. "I don't want to, Daddy. I really don't."

He lifted her, cradled her as if she were a baby again. "How about if I tuck you into bed like I used to do when you were a little girl? Remember? You'd fall asleep on the floor next to your sister, and I'd have to carry you both."

Amber put her arms around her father's neck and burrowed against his shoulder. "Yes, I remember," she whispered, longing deep inside for those golden days of her childhood. She wanted him to take her back to a place where Mommy's kisses could banish boo-boos and Daddy's presence could vanquish the things that went bump in the night. A place where children played in magic forests, where there was no darkness, only light, and where sisters did not die.

The ringing of the front doorbell intruded into Amber's dreamless sleep. Her parents had already left for work, and she had planned to go to the hospital at noon. She put the pillow over her head to muffle the sound, hoping the person would give up and go away. But the idiot wouldn't stop ringing the blasted bell. "I'm coming!" she yelled, knowing she couldn't be heard from her second-floor bedroom. She struggled into a robe and padded down the winding carpeted stairway to the foyer.

The door was made up of geometric patterns of art glass, with thick glass-block sidelights. Light streamed through, but she couldn't make out the person's idenity. "Who is it? Can you come back later?"

"A hungry traveler," the visitor answered. "Hoping you might have some peanut butter to share."

20

Amber couldn't get the door open fast enough. "Boyce!" She flung herself into his arms. "How did you—? When—?"

He pressed his fingers against her lips. "I'll tell you everything. But first . . ." He held her against his chest and kissed her until her knees went weak. He tipped his head. "You ran off before I had a chance to say something to you."

"Wh-What?"

"I love you, too."

She almost melted, then remembered they were standing in an open doorway and she was in her bathrobe. "Come inside. Give me a minute to dress. The kitchen's that way." She pointed. "The peanut butter's in the pantry, the bread's in the bread box on the counter. I'll be right back."

She flew up the stairs, jerked on clothes,

quickly brushed her teeth, began to brush her hair, and then, realizing she was losing valuable time with Boyce, tossed the brush aside and ran down to the kitchen.

He was sitting at the counter, smearing peanut butter on a slice of bread. "Found it," he said.

She stood in front of him, braced her hands on the countertop, and caught her breath. "I can't believe you came all this way just to eat my peanut butter. Why *did* you come?"

"My project in Uganda was finished, and I'm headed home. I routed myself through Miami so I could see you and Heather. I grabbed a cab from the airport."

"How long can you stay?"

"I catch a plane tonight."

"Can't you stay longer? We have plenty of room—"

"I have finals starting Monday morning. And my family's expecting me."

"Oh." She felt let down. "Did you mean what you said about loving me?"

"If you'd hadn't taken off like a scared rabbit, I would have told you in Uganda."

"Sorry. I—I've never said that to a guy before."

"Here's a tip: Don't say it and then run away." He grinned. "I'm glad I was first."

She noticed he didn't say, *"You're also the first for me."* "Well, at least you're here now. Heather's going to be thrilled to see you."

"Tell me what's going on with her."

"She's in liver failure. She's on the transplant list, but—" Amber hated to tell him how hopeless it was. She stared down at his large rough hand covering hers and began to cry. "Sh-She's not going to make it, Boyce."

He was beside her in a second and holding her in his arms. "I want to tell her goodbye."

"We'll go to the hospital as soon as you're ready."

"I'm ready," he said. "Let's go."

She told the nurses in the ICU he was a cousin, just passing through. They gave her no argument. Amber helped him put on the protective clothing and took him inside Heather's room.

Heather's eyes widened when she saw him. "Boyce? I—I don't believe it."

If he was shocked by her appearance, he didn't show it. "I don't know how you recognized me in this outfit."

"I'd know those eyes anywhere."

"You look beautiful."

"Liar. I know how bad I look."

"You'll always be beautiful to me, Heather Barlow."

"Boyce is on his way home," Amber said. "He just came by to say . . . hello. Right, Boyce?" She'd almost slipped.

Heather's gaze softened. "Just passing through, huh?"

"I can catch a plane from Miami just as easily as from Atlanta. Except I didn't know anyone in Atlanta."

"I'm glad you came. Seeing you reminds me of last summer. It was the best time, the happiest time of my whole life."

"I think of Ian, too," Boyce said automatically, as if he'd read her mind. "He was my friend, and I miss him."

"I look forward to seeing him again. And I know I will. Soon." Heather's gaze drifted to Amber. "My family's the only reason I've been holding on so hard."

Amber felt a shiver of fear.

Boyce took Heather's hand. "Is there anything I can do for you?"

"Yes. Look after my sister."

"If she'll let me."

"She's stubborn."

"Hey, you two," Amber broke in. "I'm standing right here, you know. I'm hearing every word you're saying."

"She's also vocal." Boyce winked at Heather. "What else can I do for you?"

"Pray with me."

Still holding her hand and without hesitation, Boyce knelt on the floor and bowed his head. Self-consciously Amber dropped beside him. Certainly she'd prayed with him when they'd been on the run. They'd asked God for protection, and for deliverance, and had received both. Now she wanted Boyce to beg God for Heather's life. Perhaps Boyce had more clout with God than she did. Instead, he asked God to give Heather peace and comfort. And he asked God to give her family courage and strength.

When he had finished, he stood. "Put in a good word for me when you meet the Big Guy."

Heather nodded. "Only if you'll remove that stupid mask and kiss me goodbye."

Boyce lifted the mask and pressed his lips to her forehead. "Go with God, Heather."

"You too."

Amber choked back tears.

Heather looked at her and said, "Will you two please go have some fun? I need to get some sleep."

"I'll see you later, sis," Amber said.

"Later," Heather whispered, and closed her eyes.

Numbly Amber followed Boyce out of her sister's room.

Night fell like a purple veil, and Amber drove Boyce to the airport. Once he had checked in, she waited with him inside a restaurant for his flight to be called. They were tucked back in a corner booth that overlooked the tarmac, and she could see jets taking off in the distance. They reminded her of lumbering cows as they gathered speed, of svelte giant birds once they freed themselves from the bonds of Earth and rose skyward. Boyce ordered coffee for them both.

"I'm glad you stopped off," she said. "I'm glad you talked to Heather. I could see it meant a lot to her. And it meant a lot to me, too."

"I know it's hard to lose her. She's lucky to have such a good family around her during all this."

"If I could stop time, I would."

Boyce stirred his coffee. "Amber, stopping time would only prolong her suffering. Is that what you want?"

She shook her head, struggling to control her emotions.

"I've seen people die in Africa. In Kenya we buried a baby that was only days old. If that baby had gotten sick in this country, a pediatrician could have saved her with a phone call to a drugstore. That's not the way things are over there. I think that's why people like Paul and Jodene work so hard to spread the Gospel, so that the people have some kind of comfort when they face death day after day. Knowing that heaven is waiting makes it easier on everyone, especially on those left behind."

He paused, stared pensively out the window. Out on the tarmac, a jumbo jet coasted toward a docking gate. "Amber, the worst thing that can happen to a person isn't dying. Everybody dies. The worst thing is to be separated from the love of God."

"I know I'm being selfish," Amber confessed. "But I look at the future and I can't imagine it without her. I don't know what I'm going to do when she's gone."

"You'll find your way through it because you're strong. I know that because of the time we spent together in the bush. You showed a lot of determination, a lot of grit. You're smart, too."

"So smart that I ran from our rescuers and almost got shot."

"You had no way of knowing who those men were. And when they talked about it later, they said you ran in the opposite direction from where we were located. That's loyalty, Amber."

"I—I didn't want you all to get hurt."

He reached across the table and laced his fingers through hers. "It took courage."

"So what do I do after Heather's gone? Do you have any answers for me? Because I don't think loyalty, courage, and determination are worth much if there's nothing to focus them on."

"When you go to college, something will grab your attention and you'll go after it with the same kind of single-mindedness that you showed in Africa. It's out there waiting for you to discover."

She blew her nose on a paper napkin. "Are you telling me we won't see each other again?"

"I'm telling you that as much as I'd like that

right now, I'll only be in your way. I'd be a distraction. You have to work out your future for yourself. You're right on the edge, Amber. It's there. You're here." He drew imaginary lines on the table. "Go get it."

His green eyes bore into hers, challenging her to reach for something she still couldn't visualize. Her future might look shining to him, but she saw only a dark pit. She had no plans. She had no dreams. She didn't know where to find them. "Will you wait for me?"

He drew her hand to his lips and kissed the backs of her fingers. "I'll wait."

She felt as if her heart was breaking. She was losing her sister, losing him, too, in a way. He knew the path he was walking. She still had to find hers. What if it took too long? What if someone else came along he liked better? What if he got tired of waiting for her?

"It's time for me to go," Boyce said after glancing at his watch.

"I'll walk you to your gate."

"No. Go back to the hospital. You've got to finish this chapter of your life before you can move on to the next."

He stood, scooped up his backpack, and kissed her mouth. "Remember, I love you. I would have told you that in Uganda, but you beat me to it."

She followed him to the restaurant entrance, watched him step into the passing crowd. She watched until he melted into the flow of fellow travelers heading for the rest of their lives.

Twenty-four hours later, Heather slipped into a coma, where she lived for another day before God called her home and the doctor turned off her life support.

That afternoon Amber sent an old-fashioned telegram to Paul and Jodene in Uganda, since they had no fax, no phone, no Internet service. The message read:

```
Heather went to be with the
Lord this morning, 10 AM STOP
She hurts no more STOP
She is with Ian now STOP
I miss her STOP Forever END
```

21

Amber leaned out over the ship's railing and watched the bow of the great white ship cut through the water like a giant steel blade. The ship had been under way all day, leaving London in fog and drizzle. Out here on the high seas, the overcast skies were finally breaking up and sun was streaking through the billowing gray clouds like fingers raking through soil.

"Careful. It's a long way down."

Amber turned and saw a brown-eyed girl about her age. "Don't worry. I've got a grip on the rail."

The girl rested her elbows beside Amber's hands and lifted her face to the breeze. Her brown hair tumbled away from her face. "Don't you just love the smell of the sea? I think I've been looking forward to this more than actually getting to Africa." She turned toward Amber and smiled. "I'm Sherri Dickerson, from Greenbrier, Arkansas. I'd never seen the ocean until I got on this ship. I can't believe there's so much water! Just sky and water . . . everywhere you look."

Amber introduced herself. She didn't want to be impolite, but she wished Sherri would go away. She wanted to be alone.

"This is my first time on a Mercy Ship. How about you?" Sherri asked.

"First time for me, too."

"I've been wanting to travel to Africa all my life, and when the youth pastor at my church started telling us about how he went on this ship when he was a teenager, well, I knew that was just what I wanted to do." Sherri slapped the rail for emphasis. "You too?"

"I've been to Africa before."

"You have?" Sherri looked impressed. "When?"

"Last year. I went with my mother to Uganda. She's a doctor. I stayed for almost eight weeks. And I never thought I'd ever go back."

"Uganda! That's where I'm going as part of Dr. Henry's team." Sherri's smile widened.

Amber was part of the same team, but she didn't tell Sherri. The girl would find out soon enough when they had their first shipboard meeting as a group the next morning.

A year had passed since Heather's death. A tough year for Amber. She'd kept her promise to her father and enrolled in the local junior college in September because the freshman class was full at the University of Miami, her first choice. She hadn't minded. She lived at home, went to classes, worked part-time in a shoe store, saw a few high-school friends who had opted to remain in Miami.

"What's Uganda like?" Sherri asked. "I've read about it, but you're the first person I've actually talked to who's gone there."

"Uganda's beautiful. Lots of wide-open spaces. Except in Kampala. It's a big city with a million people and one traffic light."

"You're teasing me, aren't you?"

Amber wasn't, but she didn't want a long, drawn-out conversation with this girl, so she shrugged. "You'll see."

"How about the people? Did you like the people? Mama says I'm a people person, but I'm really sort of shy. I mean, what do you talk about with people who live so different from us?"

"The people are the best part," Amber said, thinking about Ruth and Patrick. "You'll never meet better people anyplace." She'd written them after Heather's funeral, telling them about her sorrow, that she felt like crying all the time. Ruth had responded, "God uses the tears of suffering to cause growth in the gardens of our lives. This is a strange thing, but it is true. I would not be the woman I am today if not for what I suffered in my past. God will be with you, *rafiki*. He will cause you to grow in your season."

"So why are you going back? Is it because you met someone over there?" Sherri brushed away the hair that blew into her eyes.

"I met lots of people. So will you, and you'll care about them even if you don't think you will."

Boyce had called Amber and sent numerous e-mails. He was doing well in school and expected to graduate at the end of the summer term. She would be in Uganda when he did. He would start work for his father immediately. His name would go on the door of the firm in gold letters. She was proud of him.

Proud to know him. Proud to have loved him. She did still.

"Is that why you're going back? To be with the people you met before?"

Along with the other members of Dr. Henry's team, Amber would stay with Paul and Jodene. She was pleased about that part. And they were really looking forward to her coming. But that wasn't why she was returning. "No," she told Sherri. "I'm going because I must."

Sherri looked puzzled. "I don't get it. Why must you?"

Her parents had asked the same question. They had begged her to rethink her decision. She was their only child. What if something happened to her? What about college? Was she just dropping out? She was only eighteen. What was she thinking?

She'd tried to explain to them how she'd been adrift for months and just going through the motions of living, of belonging. She loved them, but she wanted to fulfill her destiny. And somehow she knew it lay not in living in her sister's shadow, but in following in her footsteps and finding a path that belonged only to Amber.

She looked into Sherri's eyes. "My sister once told me, 'Sometimes you have to do it before you feel it.' That's why I went to Africa the first time—just to do it. Now I'm going because I feel it. More than anything, I want to go."

"Oh," Sherri said, her expression one of confusion. She brightened. "Well, I hope we can be friends."

"*Rafiki*. That's 'friend' in Swahili."

Sherri repeated the word. "Cool . . . now I know some Swahili." A bell sounded. "Dinner." Sherri stepped away from the rail. "You coming?"

"In a minute. Will you save me a seat?"

"Will do."

She left, and Amber turned back to the open sea. This dark blue water was much different from the pale green surf along the shores of Miami's beaches, but they were one and the same ocean. She breathed in the salty, briny scent and turned her face skyward, toward the lead-colored clouds shot through with shafts of sunlight.

All at once the clouds divided and, like stars falling from space, two gulls swooped downward. Amber thought it odd that the birds should be so far from land, but she watched them soar and dip and glide like graceful ballerinas, untethered to the earth as she was. And she envied them. They seemed so joyous as they danced with the wind, these feathered wind sprites, these wayward vagabonds. They were together, yet separate, a pair dancing in perfect unison to the music of a song only they knew.

Perhaps Heather and Ian were together in the same way in heaven, soaring with the angels. The thought gave Amber great comfort.

The gulls dipped low across the bow of the ship, so close she could almost reach out and touch them. Then their graceful wings began to flap and they rose through a shaft of sunlight into the bank of clouds and disappeared. She stared at the sky for a long time, but they did not reappear.

But their wind dance had moved something inside her heart. Like the lid of a hinged box, her heart seemed to open, and the heaviness that had weighed her down for months lifted. Surely the gulls had been an omen, a sign from God that she was not alone. The birds were free, just as she was free. Her childhood was over, but she was beginning the greatest adventure known to her kind—an adventure called *life*.

Amber opened her arms and lifted them heavenward, as if to hold the wind, as if to hug the sky.

You can read Heather Barlow's story in
Angel of Mercy, the companion to *Angel of Hope*.

Heather Barlow has always been idealistic, and now that she has finished high school, she's ready to make a difference in the world. After graduation she joins a mission group on a hospital Mercy Ship sailing to Africa. Once she has left the ship on the Kenyan coast and is stationed at a hospital in Uganda, however, Heather is unprepared to face the disease, famine, and misery she encounters.

Ian McCollum is also among the medical staff in Uganda. Ian has left his native Scotland and combined his idealism with a career in medicine, helping those threatened by a world of seeming indifference. When Heather meets Ian her heart quickens and she feels happy to be alive. But as the weeks pass, Heather finds her idealism vanishing; the refugee camps and orphanages are overcrowded, and misery is everywhere. Only Ian can see beyond the horror and help Heather understand that the world can be changed if people try to help those in need one by one.

Lurlene McDaniel began writing inspirational novels about teenagers facing life-altering situations when her son was diagnosed with juvenile diabetes. "I saw firsthand how chronic illness affects every aspect of a person's life," she has said. "I want kids to know that while people don't get to choose what life gives to them, they do get to choose how they respond."

Lurlene McDaniel's novels are hard-hitting and realistic, but also leave readers with inspiration and hope. Her books have received acclaim from readers, teachers, parents, and reviewers. Her recent novels *Angels Watching Over Me* and its companions, *Lifted Up by Angels* and *Until Angels Close My Eyes,* have all been national bestsellers, as have *Don't Die, My Love; I'll Be Seeing You;* and *Till Death Do Us Part. Six Months to Live* was included in a literary time capsule at the Library of Congress in Washington, D.C.

Lurlene McDaniel's other popular Bantam books include *Angel of Mercy,* the companion to *Angel of Hope; The Girl Death Left Behind; Starry, Starry Night: Three Holiday Stories; For Better, for Worse, Forever; Too Young to Die; Goodbye Doesn't Mean Forever; Somewhere Between Life and Death; Time to Let Go; Now I Lay Me Down to Sleep; When Happily Ever After Ends; Baby Alicia Is Dying;* and the One Last Wish novels: *A Time to Die; Mourning Song; Mother,*

Help Me Live; Someone Dies, Someone Lives; Sixteen and Dying; Let Him Live; The Legacy: Making Wishes Come True; Please Don't Die; She Died Too Young; All the Days of Her Life; A Season for Goodbye; and *Reach for Tomorrow.*

Lurlene McDaniel lives in Chattanooga, Tennessee.

If you are interested in learning more about the Mercy Ship ministry, please contact:

Youth with a Mission
MERCY SHIPS
P.O. Box 2020
Lindale, TX 75771-2020